WHAT BURNS

WHAT BURNS

STORIES

DALE PECK

SOHO

Published by Soho Press
227 W 17th Street
New York, NY 10011

Library of Congress Cataloging-in-Publication Data

Peck, Dale, author.
What burns : stories / Dale Peck.

ISBN 978-1-64129-082-1
eISBN 978-1-64129-083-8

LCC PS3566.E245 A6 2019 (print) I LCC PS3566.E245 (ebook)
DDC 813/.54—dc23

Interior design by Janine Agro, Soho Press, Inc.

Printed in the United States of America

10 9 8 7 6 5 4 3 2 1

Science, like philosophy, has sought to escape from the doctrine of perpetual flux by finding some permanent substratum amid changing phenomena. Chemistry seemed to satisfy this desire. It was found that fire, which appears to destroy, only transmutes: elements are recombined, but each atom that existed before combustion still exists when the process is completed. Accordingly it was supposed that atoms are indestructible, and that all change in the physical world consists merely in rearrangement of persistent elements. This view prevailed until the discovery of radioactivity, when it was found that atoms could disintegrate.

Nothing daunted, the physicists invented new and smaller units, called electrons and protons, out of which atoms were composed; and these units were supposed, for a few years, to have the indestructibility formerly attributed to atoms. Unfortunately it seemed that protons and electrons could meet and explode, forming, not new matter, but a wave of energy spreading through the universe with the velocity of light. Energy had to replace matter as what is permanent. But energy, unlike matter, is not a refinement of the common-sense notion of a "thing"; it is merely a characteristic of physical processes. It might be fancifully identified with the Heraclitean Fire, but it is the burning, not what burns. "What burns" has disappeared from modern physics.

—Bertrand Russell

WHAT BURNS

Contents

I.

I know everything. Names, places, dates. The number of the dead and the location of the bodies. The secret histories of love and war and the tally of coins fallen behind the cushion. When you were a baby your mother called you by a name not even your father knew, and then she died. When you were twenty-seven you finally shared that name with the woman you'd asked to marry you. For weeks afterward you kept thinking about how the word sounded on her lips—it was the first time you'd heard it spoken aloud since you were four—when, tenderly, she turned you down. That was eleven years ago. Now you can't remember the name. I know it; I could tell you. But this and a thousand other facts will die with me, and soon.

Not Even Camping Is Like Camping Anymore

Davis was pushing a tiny wheeled cart across the living room carpet when I walked through the front door. The cart was attached to a long stick painted some pinkish red color halfway between old white lady lipstick and dog's penis. As it rolled back and forth a propeller connected to one of the axles batted a bunch of wooden balls around a clear plastic bubble like the thoughts in a crazy person's head. The cart was John Deere green and if it looked like anything it looked like a lawnmower, but Davis called it his Lectroluck, which where he picked up that word is anybody's guess. We had a Hoover, and I seriously doubt his mom even knew what a vacuum was.

Hey, Gayvis, what's up?

In my experience *gay* is one of those words, like *penis*, that's always good for a laugh. Davis, however, didn't laugh, or look up from his vacuuming. He wore an apron made from one of my T-shirts held in place by one of my belts, double wrapped around his soft tiny waist.

Well look who finally decided to come home? Would it have *killed* you to pick up a phone?

I dropped my gym bag in the middle of the floor and headed down the hall.

Blaine Gunderson! After I slaved *all day* to clean this house for you, and dinner still to get ready! The least you could do is—

I slammed my bedroom door on Davis's rant. Davis's mom worked as a waitress at the titty bar out by the interstate. She worked the day shift, when there were six, maybe seven cars in the parking lot, tops. One of them was hers, and one of them was the stripper's, and one of them was the bartender's, and plus Davis's mom was a little fat, so you know the tips sucked. My mom said flat out that the only way she could possibly make ends meet was by blowing truckers. I could see how a mother like that could drive you crazy. My mom wasn't half as bad as Davis's, and she made me nuts.

I cracked my laptop just as Davis hipped open the door, his Lectroluck clackety-clack-clacking into the room behind him, my backpack hanging off his tiny shoulders like a catamount mauling a calf.

Don't you close the door when I'm talking to you, Blaine Gunderson.

My mom wasn't very good at covering her tracks. The cache of Internet Explorer said that after she checked for updates on the gay porn site she read every day she looked up recipes for tuna casserole and green beans almondine, which turned out to be green beans with almonds. Great. Green beans *and* nuts.

Davis vacuumed my floor, his little voice barely audible above the racket. All day I slave, and do I hear one word of thanks? One Honey, the house sure looks great, or Is that a new hairstyle, darlin', or even Screw it, babe, put the pork chops back in the fridge and let's go to Olive Garden? No. *Nothing.*

Davis, if you keep pushing that toy around I'm gonna shove

that lipstick penis so far up your rectum you'll have to vacuum with your ass.

Rectum: another one of those words. Davis didn't seem to know this, but at least he dropped the penis stick and pulled his feather duster from the belt of his apron.

Was it creepy that my mom looked at gay porn? Or was it only creepy because she did it on my computer? The computer'd been a fourteenth-birthday present from my dad, which sent my mom through the roof. Can't afford child support but he can drop a thousand dollars on a computer? How'm I supposed to pay the mortgage with *that*? I doubt the computer was worth a thousand bucks new and it was beat to hell by the time I got it, but at least my dad's porn, or the porn of whoever he bought it from, was gender appropriate, even if the girls were my age.

Davis's duster flitted and fluttered over the computer screen.

Blaine! Looking at those kinds of pictures, and in front of me! Imagine!

This way I don't *have* to imagine. Hey, Gayvis, why don't you clean under the bed? Or in the closet? Or maybe on a busy highway?

Davis worked his way down the desk and reached his duster up to the windowsill. He'd had it with him the first morning his mom dropped him off at our house, and before she left he was already running it over the TV and stereo. I caught the scene as I was heading off to school: a five-year-old with a feather duster and a kerchief tied around his head, I had to stop. His right pinkie stuck out as though he held a teacup and a golden cloud enveloped him, iridescent in the morning light.

Static electricity draws dust bunnies like bees to honey!

I looked at the mother of the freak. A couple inches of stomach rolled out between her cutoffs and a Double-O Inn T-shirt. The Os circled her boobs and the INN had an arrow at the bottom of the second *N* that pointed to her vagina.

Don't you worry about Davis, she said, sucking on a cigarette. He just has his little routine.

I know how housework can get away from you, Mrs. Gunderson, Davis said, lifting a china figurine from the TV, dusting it, setting it back down. But don't you worry, I'm here now. If you'll just show me where you keep the cleaning supplies, I'll have this place spic 'n' span before you know it.

I get off at four, Davis's mom said, reaching a finger into the fold of her navel and pulling out a belly ring. But sometimes I run a little late. She let go of her belly ring and it disappeared again. I looked up to see if maybe her hair had gotten longer.

Blaine, Davis said now. I want to talk to you about your mother. I know I must sound like a broken record on this, but I'm not sure how much longer I can continue to live with *that woman*.

On screen, Tina told me she'd been saving it all for me, but I knew she hadn't.

Always with the telephone, and the TV, and the nail polish. *All day* the woman does her nails. Would it kill her to do *one load* of laundry, or even rinse her toothpaste blobbies down the sink? And our love life has suffered since she moved in. I hate to say it, Blaine, but you know it's the truth.

No, Tina hadn't saved anything. But she was willing to show

me what she'd learned from giving it away. That's what I liked about Tina.

And her friends! Don't *even* get me started on her friends.

My mom's "friends" were the other kids she babysits. This had been her brainwave last spring, which coincided with her getting canned from the café for spending more time flirting than working: unlicensed day care. Substandard service at bargain basement prices. The business didn't actually have a name, but my mom referred to it as Broken Homes, Not Broken Bones.

Meanwhile, Tina wanted me to take it out of my pants. Just then there was that knock/open thing my mom did, and her face appeared in the doorway with the phone tucked under her ear. As a well-prepared teen, my computer faced away from the door, and I glared at my mom over Tina's teased hair as if it was *me* who'd caught *her* doing something.

Davis, honey, your mom just beeped in. She's gonna be late so you'll be having dinner with us, okay? It's tuna casserole, your favorite.

Davis had clambered on the bed and was running the edge of his apron—i.e., my shirt—between the posts of my headboard.

It's not Could we have tuna casserole tonight? or even I'm feeling like tuna casserole, what about you? No, it's It's tuna casserole, *your* favorite, as though it was *my* idea all along.

Green beans almondine, honey. You'll love it.

And does she even ask what my husband, her son, who pays for the roof over her head, wants for dinner? No-o-o.

Your husband hates tuna casserole. And green beans. And nuts. Except his own, of course.

Oh, Blaine, don't encourage him, he's weird enough as it is.

With a little scrolling I was able to make Tina's face disappear, and my mom's took its place. The result looked like one of those caricatures you get at the state fair, with the head all big and the body tiny, and the boobs sticking out from either side of the skinny abdomen like balloons tied to a stick. It occurred to me that the creepiest thing about my mom looking at gay porn on my computer was that she looked up recipes immediately afterwards.

I do not like it when you look at me that way, Blaine Gunderson. You are a very disturbed boy. No, Dan, not you, she said into the phone. My other boy. And baby? The yard is looking a little raggedy. You think you could get out the mower and—not *you*, Dan. My *other* baby. She closed the door, her giggles faded down the hall. An afterimage of red nail polish hung in front of my eyes, although I couldn't remember actually seeing her hands.

Fine, I'll *make* your tuna casserole. Anything *you* want, Mother Gunderson.

I closed the laptop on Tina's headless body, swiveled the chair to face Davis. He was taking the soccer clothes out of my bag. T-shirt, shorts, socks. Despite the fact that they were soaked with sweat and caked with mud he folded them one at a time and put them in my dresser. He stopped when he came to the jock, which he held up with a questioning look on his face.

Dear?

It's the wrapper from some head cheese I bought today.

Davis put his free hand on his hip and frowned skeptically.

No, really, smell it. It smells like head cheese.

The jock was gray and kind of caky, the cup still in it. Davis brought it close to his face and his nose wrinkled. He sniffed once, then a second time. Then a third.

I don't believe I care for head cheese, dear. He threw the jock in the wastebasket beside the bed, which was mostly filled with tissues.

Oh, do you have a cold? He pawed through the wastebasket, taking out tissue after tissue and lining them up on the windowsill like sharp-edged snowballs. You should tell me these things, I could have picked up some Nyquil while you were at work. You'll be up all night. Blaine! Davis called as I walked out of the room. I *hope* you didn't forget it's Valentine's Day tomorrow!

It was July 20, 2005, seven months to the day into George W. Bush's second term of office. Davis was still five years old.

SO. MOWING THE lawn's cool, or at least it's something you can do and see what you've done—as opposed to soccer, say, which is something that's gone as soon as you do it. Don't get me wrong. I liked soccer, and camp got me out of the house during the summer, as my mom liked to say, but I didn't quite get the point of it. There was nothing to hold on to unless someone took a picture—and that's not soccer, it's just someone else's memory. And it wasn't like I enjoyed mowing the lawn or anything, though I did like the tracks of cut and uncut grass. That day I mowed the word *FUCK* into the front yard and then mowed it out. Whenever a Japanese car went by I flipped the driver the bird. I don't have anything against the Japanese, or their cars, but you have to have a system, right? Otherwise you end up hating everything.

Speaking of systems: Davis walked back and forth between the front door and the trash bin on the street. He held his apron up by the corners and carried something in the dimple with great delicacy, as though it were an unhatched egg. When he got to the bin he transferred the two corners of the apron to one hand and threw the lid open with the other—he had to heave his whole body to get the hinged lid to lift past ninety degrees and fall against the back of the bin—and then he pinched two fingers into the dimple of the apron and pulled out . . . wait for it . . . one of the tissues from my bedroom. He threw the tissue away, then turned around and repeated the process. He always closed the lid before he went back inside, and to top it off he only walked in the lines I'd mown, so that each trip took about five minutes. I appreciated his method, but god, the kid had issues. More issues than I had tissues, har har.

The whole Davis-is-my-wife thing started about a week after he began coming to our house. I got home from school and found Ari and Ina, the six-year-old Eggleston twins, sitting side by side on the couch, staring at Davis with expressions half fascinated, half paralyzed.

Ladies, Davis was saying, even though Ari was a boy, I'll tell you what my mother told me when I was your age. There are three things you need to do to keep your man. One. Never say no. It don't matter if your ankles are swollen from a double shift out to the Oh-Oh Inn and all you want is a tequila slammer and a Sominex. When the little soldier lifts his bayonet you lie down flat and take one for the team. Two. Dinner at six. Always. A full man is a sleepy man, and a sleepy man won't be out chasing tail, let alone starting a half-breed family in the trailer park on the south side of town. He is also slower on his feet. And three. Always keep your waheena clean. There is nothing that makes a man bust your lip open faster than a stenchy waheena, and believe you me, thirteen stitches take a longer time to get over than the sting of a little douche.

Ari, shy and obedient, raised his hand.

What's a *waheena*?

Ina, more worldly and dominant, elbowed Ari in the ribs.

You don't have one.

Ari looked like he was going to ask his question again, but then his eyes went wide and he clapped both hands over his mouth.

Now watch, ladies, as I demonstrate the proper way to greet your man when he comes home from a hard day at work.

Davis walked into the kitchen. The refrigerator door opened, followed by the sound of a popped top. A moment later, Davis reappeared with one of my mom's Silver Bullets. He leaned provocatively against the doorframe, one hand stretched above him so that his dirty T-shirt rode up over an inch of equally dirty belly.

Hello baby, he said in a breathy voice. Can I offer you a cold one? Or would you prefer something . . . *hot*?

Just then my mom walked in the back door.

Don't even think about it, Blaine. She pinched the beer from Davis and took a swig. Then, realizing Mrs. Eggleston was due any minute, she put the open can back in the fridge. Isn't he cute? He's been going on about you all day.

Davis regarded my mom with his hands on his hips and a disapproving frown on his face.

Really, Alice. You had him for the first fourteen years of his life. It's time to cut the cord.

Davis's mom showed up late that night, funky with booze and cigarettes, a sort of misty/smoky cloud enveloping her body, and then sharper blasts (the word *stenchy* came to mind) when she opened her mouth. A crusty stain, like brown gravy, or feces, stood out prominently on her stonewashed miniskirt.

Maybe it was because she talked so much trash behind her back, but something about Davis's mom made my mom nervous, and she stood up from the couch and held out her hand. The only time I've ever seen my mom offer someone her hand like that is to pull them out of a pool or something.

Hey, Miss Davis. Davis is all ready to go. Just let me get him.

I stood in the living room with Davis's mom. The only light came from *7th Heaven* and the tip of Davis's mom's Capri when she took a drag. There was a white mark on the left side of her upper lip, but I couldn't tell if it was a scar or just a crack in her lipstick.

You named your son Davis Davis?

Pfft. She sucked in smoke like she was doing a whip-it. *Poof.* The smoke she exhaled felt damp on my face, like it was full of spores.

I named him after his daddy.

She fixed me with a kind of dead gaze, and I should have known to drop it. But I didn't.

I didn't know you were married.

Pfft. Poof.

Who said I was married?

Suddenly a scream came from the back of the house.

I . . . said . . . in . . . a . . . MINUTE!

Oh goddamn that child! Davis's mom whirled on her wooden heels, caught her balance on the wall, then thumped heavily down the hall. Davis! Quit your fussing and get on out here!

Davis was in my bedroom. He'd dragged the chair in front of the dresser and stood on it, looking at himself in the mirror. He had my mom's hairbrush, and he was brushing his hair down the side of his face with long even strokes. He wore one of my T-shirts, which he'd made into a sort of nightgown by cinching it below his chest with something that I thought was a shoelace.

Ninety-sixteen, nineteen seventy-three, nine two nine two nine—

He says he has to do both sides a hundred times, my mom whispered.

He can't count to a hundred.

That's sort of the problem.

Davis continued brushing. His mouse-brown hair was charged with so much static electricity that it followed the brush up and down like a swarm of cobras transfixed by a flute.

Ninety-ninety, one huntert.

Davis put the brush at a perpendicular angle to the edge of the dresser. When he stepped down from the chair his nightgown rode up a little, and I could see he wasn't wearing any underwear. He looked not at his mom, or mine, but straight at me.

Ready to hit the sack, big boy?

And, sashaying, he walked the three steps to my bed and plumped the pillow invitingly. I wondered if he thought the pillow was the sack he was asking me to hit.

Nothing moved except for Davis's mom's right arm. Three puffs of smoke filled my bedroom. Finally she hung her Capri from her bottom lip and walked over and grabbed her son and swooped him onto her shoulder with one final *oof* of smoke. Davis's eyes never left mine until his mom turned around unsteadily. Inside my shirt his legs straddled her right boob, and the nipple was visible beneath her T-shirt, and mine.

He don't know what he's saying. He's just a little boy.

A thin singsong filled the room. It was Davis, singing "Fever" in a falsetto whisper.

When you put your harms around me

His staticky hair shot straight out from his head and attached itself to his mom's as though thoughts were passing between them via wires.

Penis, I said.

Davis giggled.

AN INCESSANT HONKING drove me to the kitchen, where I found my mom's boyfriend, Dan, sitting in front of a children's toy that was basically the dashboard of a car, complete with steering wheel and electronic horn. This wasn't as strange as it sounds. No, nix that. It was every bit as strange as it sounds. Dan, you see, spent all his spare time "adapting" famous riffs from classical music for the horn of his 1999 Renault Something or Other, which he thought would get him on TV one day (Why, yes, Regis, I *do* play an instrument: the French horn). So you know, first of all, that he's *a winner*, and, secondly, that his neighbors *love him* (the toy, in fact, was a "gift" from one of them, who heaved the box through his living room window). That night he was practicing something he called "Also Sprach Zarathustra," which nonpretentious people know as the theme to *2001*. The steering wheel was smaller than his hand, and, what with the intense look of concentration on his face and his wild hair—bushy and uncombed on the sides but thin on top—he looked like a circus clown in a midget car. His "fondness" for Hawaiian shirts didn't help, especially since most of them were "pre-owned." With Dan you had to use a lot of quotation marks.

The clock over the sink read a quarter past eight.

Dan? Hey, Dan? Dan? Dan? Dan? Dan? Dan? Dan? Dan?

Dan finally looked up. There was an innocent expression on his face, as if he was surprised to find that he wasn't alone.

Huh?

Open the pod bay doors, Dan.

Dan blinked.

Huh?

He means the horn, honey, my mom said in the kind of voice you'd use to talk to a five-year-old. Playtime's over, dear, it's time for din-din. She turned from the oven holding the casserole in mitted hands. Stopped.

Huh.

What? Dan said.

Davis only set two places at the table. Davis? Honey, where are you anyway?

He turned out to be in the dining room, where he'd set two more places, complete with paper napkins his little fingers had folded into convincingly birdlike shapes, and a few bits of clover blossom in a glass, and a candle, lit. Because the table was so high, he was kneeling on his chair instead of sitting on it. He looked like an altar boy at a shrine. There was something worshipful in his expression.

Blaine? Darling? I thought tonight we could renew our vows.

Davis, I told you not to play with matches. My mom blew the candle out, spattering wax over the tabletop. Now come on, grab your plate and come in the kitchen with the rest of us. Blaine, grab your plate.

In the kitchen, Dan had replaced his toy with a beer. There was a crunching sound as his spoon broke the crust on the top of my mom's tuna casserole.

My mom smiled hopefully. The recipe called for just a little bit of dirty sock cheese sprinkled over the top. I was afraid it would make it less crispy but it seems to have worked out okay.

Dan systematically skimmed off the top layer of casserole, which everyone knows is the best part, and put it all on his plate. He pushed the gloopy remainder in front of me.

Here you go, Bland, dig in.

Bland was Dan's idea of a joke.

Dan was a bit of a jokester.

He watched intently as I spooned noodles on my plate. My mom'd been seeing him for about a year at that point, which was pretty much a record for her. I'd managed to stay out of his way, mostly, because he preferred to take my mom back to his place to screw, mostly. A lot of times he just sat in his car and honked, usually "Shave and a Haircut" or the Woody Woodpecker song, but sometimes he treated us to a couple of bars of Beethoven's Fifth or Ninth, or the Lone Ranger theme, which I have to admit he played amazingly well. When he did stay I usually left, or went to bed.

A few drops of cream of mushroom soup spilled on the table.

Oh, Bland, look at that! Looks like you could use . . . a *tissue*. With a flourish, Dan pulled one from the breast pocket of his Hawaiian shirt.

My mom stifled a snort, barely.

Blaine has the sniffles, Davis said, snapping the tissue from Dan's fingers and blotting up the soup. He *also* has all his hair.

My mom let the second snort fly.

The things that come out of that boy's mouth! She pulled his plate towards her and scooped casserole and green beans onto it. It's almost eerie how grown-up he sounds.

If you ask me, what was eerie about Davis wasn't that he talked the way he did, but that he talked the way he did and still managed to pick up on what was happening in the part of the world that existed outside his weird little brain. For example: my mom's nails. They were, in fact, freshly painted. Not red, as I'd thought, but purple.

Why thank you, Alice, Davis said when my mom slid his plate back in front of him. And then: It's so nice to see you helping out around here. Now that *Blaine*'s home.

My mom's grin hardened. Like I said. The things that come out of that boy's mouth. She spooned green beans onto Dan's plate, mine, then served herself. Shut up, Blaine. You'll understand when you have kids of your own.

Alice raises a good point, Davis said. When *are* we going to have children of our own?

Dan got up, got a second beer from the fridge.

I mean really, Blaine. What do we do it all for, if not to leave it to the next generation? It won't mean nothing to us when we're dead and gone.

Standing behind Davis, Dan made the universal symbol for crazy over his head.

Is it a crime that I want to have children, Blaine? Davis pushed his plate in front of my mom. Load me up, Alice, tonight I start eatin' for two.

Dan returned to his chair, set his beer down heavily on the table.

Why don't you start with that, Davis? my mom said. If you want seconds, there's plenty.

But Davis was looking at me, his face as round and deep and full as my mom's casserole pot. I wanna have triplets and name them all after you: *Buh-lay-un*. C'mon, baby. Stick a bun in my oven. Knock me up. Get me in the family way. Take me right now, on the kitchen table. Let's do it like teenagers!

Davis! my mom said. *Blaine* is a teenager. *You* are five years old.

Dan was staring at Davis with a look of fascination and

disgust. What really bugged me, though, was that I knew the same expression was on my face.

Good Christ. What uncle fucked that little boy?

Dan's dumb-ass comment made me think about what Davis's mom had said that one time—about Davis being named after his daddy—but my thoughts were cut off by a smack. My mom's hand, Dan's cheek. Not particularly loud, not particularly hard, but apparently hard enough to piss him off. Before either of us knew what was happening he was holding my mom's wrists in one hand, squeezing her jaw with the other. Her fork clattered to the floor.

When I think of a new life growing inside of me! Oh, Blaine! I know that's what god put me here for! To bring a little love into the world!

Uh, Dan. You wanna let go of my mom?

Shut up, Blaine. This is between your mom and me.

If there were more loving homes in the world, there'd be less violence. Less war. We could start a revolution, Blaine. You and me. Right here, in our own home.

Uh, Dan? I made a little knocking sound on the table, and Dan looked over to see that I had my knife in my hand. That's really not cool.

Out of the corner of my eye I could see Davis rubbing his belly with one hand. Full men rub their bellies vigorously with their whole hand, but pregnant women only use their fingertips, only touch gently, as if afraid to wake the child slumbering within. As with everything else, Davis got the details perfect. Only the body was wrong.

Dan let go of my mom and settled back into his chair. Jesus

Christ, Blaine, calm down. It wasn't nothing. He picked up his beer and drained it in one long glugging gulp.

My mom unfolded her napkin into her lap. I'm sorry I hit you, Dan. But you shouldn't talk that way about Davis. Especially not in front of him. Blaine, she added, picking up her napkin and patting her lips, although she hadn't started eating yet. Put the knife down, please.

Dan burped, and then he picked up his fork and began shoveling a green-and-gray mixture of tuna casserole and green beans into his mouth. Somebody should get that boy help.

It was unclear whether he meant me or Davis. My mom looked at me and then she looked at Davis, as if trying to decide.

Jesus fucking Christ, she said finally. Where the hell *is* that woman? Her eyes looked at the left side of her plate, the right. Not seeing her fork, she picked up her spoon and started eating. It was a teaspoon, so she was forced to take Davis-sized bites.

Davis had already finished eating, and held his plate out for seconds. I wondered if he thought being pregnant just meant you got fat.

BUT DAVIS'S MOM didn't come, and at ten o'clock, with Davis curled up next to me on the couch—Dan was already in bed—my mom said it was time both of us hit the hay.

He can bunk with you.

Aw, Mom. Why can't he sleep on the couch?

My mom looked around our living room. Some rundown places look better in dim light, but ours looked worse: the shadows in the warped paneling seemed like actual holes, and the upstretched arms on the dancing figurines my mom "collected" (she found a box of them at a garage sale and bought the whole set for ten bucks) looked like sinners running from the second coming. The picture frames on top of the TV were dark rectangles, and at this point I can't even remember whose faces hid inside them.

He's five years old. That's just too depressing.

It'll be like camping.

My mom shook her head. Not even camping is like camping anymore. Now take a pillow from my bed. Preferably the one Dan's using.

I carried him down the hall. I was surprised by how light he was. I wasn't a big kid, wasn't particularly strong, but Davis felt lighter than the pillow I tugged from beneath Dan's snoring head. Dan didn't wake up at the jerking motion, but Davis did, and when his unfocused eyes squinted in my direction I remember I wanted him to say something that'd make it clear the whole Davis-in-an-apron thing was just an act. That he knew who he really was. Who *I* really was. Instead he curled his arms around my neck and turned his face into my chest and whispered, *Finally.*

I pulled his shorts off him, laid him on the outer edge of the bed, then got undressed and climbed over him to the side next to the wall. I figured it was better he had the outside, in case he had to pee in the middle of the night. I realized I'd forgotten to give him his pillow, which sat on my dresser, on top of my laptop. Circuits crossed, fired, fizzled: the pillow from my mom's bed, the laptop with its pictures of Tina, Davis's whistling breath on my right side, the cold flat wall pressing against my left shoulder. I mean, Jesus Christ, who needs to look up a recipe for *tuna casserole*?

Voices came from the other side of the wall:

Who took my pillow?

I'll take your pillow, mister.

Aw, baby, you're not still mad? You know I didn't mean nothing. A pause. That kid gives me the creeps. It's really *got* to come from somewhere.

Oh, Dan. Dan, Dan, Dan.

What? What, what, what?

If you were a parent, Dan, you wouldn't care where it came from. You'd care where it was going.

Let's face it: the reason I didn't want Davis to sleep in my room was because nighttime was when I jerked off. My penis poked above the waistband of my boxers like a loaf of French bread sticking out of a grocery bag. I tried lying on my back but the blanket seemed to caress the tip. I tried lying on my stomach but the heavy weight of my body made me want to grind my hips into the bed. I turned on my side, and there was Davis, all of four inches away, and that was just weird. I turned to face the wall. I tried angling my penis so that it lay under the waistband of my boxers, and it popped out of the fly. Apparently my penis didn't like being angled. I tried to think of the severed heads of chicken, the hair in the bathtub drain, the motherboard in my computer. Apparently my penis was not put off by abstract thought. I found myself wondering how the French got their bread home without busting the loaf in half: it bumped against *everything*.

Penis, I whispered, and laughed at my own joke.

The stereo went on in the other room. *Hooked on Classics*, Dan's favorite camouflage. In approximately seven minutes he would patter out a bit of "Eine Kleine Nachtmusik" or "Rhapsody in Blue" on the bedside table. If nothing else, his presence in our lives had been educational.

A few inches behind me, Davis turned. His breath came louder, and I realized he was facing me. In the quiet, his silent voice was strangely present, a singsong bouncing back and forth between my ears to the accompaniment of the creaking bedsprings in the next room. Davis's words, the things he talked about doing, were a pretty straightforward imitation of the women in his life—his mom, and, let's face it, mine—crossed with women he saw on TV. The fifties sitcoms Nickelodeon ran ad infinitum, with their bright-faced beaming slaves in starched aprons and permanent waves, and the ones on my mom's soaps, who were a different kind of caricature, all sucked, tucked, fucked. The combination could only be called freaky, especially when it came wrapped up in a five-year-old boy's impossibly tiny, incredibly fragile body. I remembered the weightless weight of him in my arms. Was I ever that small, I wondered. Was my mom? Dan? It seemed impossible that someone like Dan could've passed through such a stage before turning into his adult self, omnivorous, with a bladder that could hold a quart of urine and fingers that bruised, broke, smudged, and made music from the strangest sources.

Sometimes I felt like Dan. I wanted there to be a revelation, a single incident to explain away Davis's behavior. The uncle or grandpa teaching Davis things he was too young to know, an overabundance of some chemical in his brain. But as far as I knew there was nothing like that. Aside from the general fucked-upedness of his existence, I mean, which was no more fucked up than mine or anybody else's that I knew, there was no abuse, sexual or otherwise, no traumatic witnessings, no blows to the head. It seemed that Davis just knew what he wanted. That he was one of the few people in this world who wasn't afraid to ask for it.

As if reading my mind, Davis sighed. His whisper wasn't all fake sexy like the voice I'd been hearing in my head. It sounded like the voice of a little boy whose mom'd forgot about him a long time ago.

Blaine? Please?

You shut your cakehole, Davis. Just shut your fucking mouth.

See, the thing is, I wasn't like Davis. I couldn't let my mind go far away like he could and still keep track of the world around me. But when I tried to focus on the things that were right next to me, they ended up losing their edges a bit, and the next thing I knew there was a knife in my hand. Or a penis. Or my mom: why was it that she looked at pictures of gay guys who were all hairless and oiled and curved like, well, like really hard women, but then she went and picked a guy like Dan out of the lineup, whose only curve was his beer gut, and hair everywhere but where it was supposed to be? What I mean is, how come he made her happy, when she seemed to want something else?

Sniffles now. Little bitty sobs. I did my best to think about Tina, then realized my hand was moving in time to the creaks in the next room. And the music: Barber's *Adagio for Strings*. Who in the hell fucks to something that's basically a war requiem? And then suddenly a drum roll, so loud I jumped and rolled away:

Bah-dah bah-bah-bah, I'm lovin' it!

I realized I was facing Davis. In the dark, I couldn't tell if his eyes were open or closed, only that they were wet. His hands were folded under his cheek in the universal symbol of sleep and prayer, I could feel his breath on my face, and all I could think was, how do you tell a five-year-old that he's made it impossible for anyone to touch him? But then I thought, what *do* we do it all for, if not for the next generation?

Aw, fuck it, Davis. C'mere.

Reader, I made him so happy it nearly killed us both.

—2010

II.

From my window I can hear the bells of the Orthodox church and see the rising glass curve of the building they finally managed to erect on Astor Place. Friday and Saturday nights there are the sounds and smells of McSorley's, and once a year the Ukrainian festival wafts in: roasting sausage, sauerkraut tang, tinny PAs distorting a language fewer and fewer people understand on this street. The new building's the future of the neighborhood. It looks down on sharp-chinned Irish drunks and round-cheeked Slavic congregants, but its oil-slick panes tilt upward, to reflect the sky. The window frames break the image, so that it looks less like a mirror than a bank of television monitors, and the clouds they reflect seem to come from inside the empty building. The building thinks: I will outlast you, *but it doesn't say if its* you *refers to me or the clouds. It's not interesting enough to claim it will outlast me: the starlings hatching in the rusted cornice of the building across the street will live longer than I will. No, like all 'scrapers, this building hates the sky.*

Bliss

My mother's killer was named Waters. The morning he was released from prison was sharp and hazy, a spring day with a scattering of leftover clouds that dotted the sky like shredded bits of tissue paper floating in water. Everything seemed overdetermined that morning, all the details right out of that scene in the movie where The Killer Is Released. The shapeless clouds, the crisp diamond lattice of the fence through which I saw them, the fat gate guard, his uniform stretched so taut across the gelid curves of his body that it seemed to cry out for the pierce of bullet or knife. Black puddles reflected the limestone walls of the prison until a car traveling the length of the parking lot spat grit into them, causing the walls to disappear. Then the water stilled, revealing the image of Shenandoah Waters. He was dressed in stiff jeans and a chambray shirt faded nearly white, the sleeves rolled up over arms nearly as faded, and etched by pale blue veins and razor-blade-and-Bic-ink tattoos of Jesus, Mary, and a snarling Ford pickup. Over one shoulder hung the slack green lozenge of an Army-issue duffel bag, and this bag slapped audibly against Shenandoah Waters's backside as he walked resolutely towards the open gate. Between the gate's pillars he paused, as the freed do. He took a deep breath. He grinned nervously at the security guard, and then he squinted through the thick-lensed black-framed glasses that covered his eyes like a bandit's mask—a new pair since the last time I'd seen him—then started forward again, the *slap-a-dap* slap of the duffel bag coming at a slightly faster rhythm. As he reached my car I pressed a button that rolled down the passenger side window with a loud squeal. Shenandoah Waters started; nineteen years in prison hadn't made him any less jumpy. He leaned down and peered at me through his glasses, and the cut planes of his freshly shaved face filled the empty window. A thin line of stubble traced the subcutaneous arc of his right jawbone. It was so close to my eyes that had I wanted to I could have counted the individual hairs.

I counted; there were sixteen, seven of which were gray. I smiled.

Want a ride?

ON THE MORNING after Shenandoah Waters killed my mother the sky was suitably gray, the clouds thick and portentous as a roll of toilet paper knocked in the bowl. They were just squeezing out their first drops as my father let me off at the edge of our yard, and I ran up the sidewalk and ducked into the house and even as I lifted my head to call her name I saw her on the floor at the foot of the stairs. The only blood on her body was a tiny spot below her left nostril. It was the size of the eraser on a new pencil, and it had bubbled up like yeasted bread before hardening into a brown scab. In the six or so hours since her death the rest of her body had stiffened too—not the skin, which had a Play-Dohy pliability, nor the bones, which seemed if anything to have softened, but something between the two. The first thing I tried to do was raise her head but her neck wouldn't bend. Then I tried to pull her hand to mine but it wouldn't come away from her body. It was only after I saw a strange pair of black glasses lying a few feet away that I ran outside to see if my father was still there, but he'd already driven off. The rain seemed to have solidified in the air, and fell without making any noise on the lawn.

Twenty years ago, Kansas: five-year-old boys weren't taught *911*. Five-year-olds were taught their names and addresses and phone numbers, they were taught *If I'm not here turn the TV on and wait for me to come home and only one pop before supper.* I went inside and shut the door. I didn't turn the television on but I did drink a can of pop even though it was only seven in the morning, and by the time the can was empty my mother's arm had softened up enough for me to pull her still-stiff fingers into my lap. The sleeve of her black plastic raincoat rustled when I moved her arm, and I didn't like the feel of it in my hands. I thought of taking it off but I only got as far as unzipping it. Underneath my mother wore her favorite pale pink dress, still belted at the waist with a thin gold buckle but ripped open at the throat where two buttons had popped off during her fall down the stairs, and atop her breastbone, twisted into a lazy figure eight, was a thin string of pearls. It was the pearls that stopped me. Their double loop— one curled around her neck, the other framing a patch of fading summer tan—seemed too delicate to disturb, and I forgot about removing the raincoat and reached instead for my pop. It was empty save for a single syrupy drop, and when it fell on my tongue I nearly gasped, and I held it there for a long time before swallowing. Held it until I could shake the idea that it was one of my mother's pearls I was swallowing.

The only thing that seemed to explain what I did after that was *wait for me to come home*, and I did, and it wasn't until late in the afternoon, when the school had called my father's house after calling my mother's several times, *and whatever you do don't pick up the phone*, that he came over and found us, her hand in mine, the empty can of pop, the eraserhead of dried blood—and the black glasses, which I still don't remember putting on, dangling off the end of my nose. It may seem horrific and who knows, maybe it was, but fifteen years of passive recollection and another five of active retelling at Group have changed these memories into little more than scenic details, stock phrases I choose whether or not to voice. That's what they teach us in Group: we can choose to tell or not tell our stories, we can impose our own meanings on them rather than letting them have power over us. In Group they teach us to love what we hate. They teach us that the only way to stop hating is to turn it into love, blame has nothing to do with it they teach us, and, like you, the first time I heard such absurdities I laughed. I couldn't help myself, and I tried to hide it behind my hand, but still: I laughed.

The woman before me had been talking about her husband, whom she'd found in a pool of his own blood. She didn't call it a *pool*: she called it a *gel*. She'd told this story so often she'd had time to replace the word *pool* with *gel* and *blood* with *essence*, and the knife that she called a *dagger* was stuck in the nineteenth of thirty-three stab wounds that left her husband's skin *no more solid than the walls of Jericho come tumbling down*. Walter had told her that. Walter had told her it wasn't until the thirty-third thrust that he realized what he was doing, at which point he began reinserting the knife into each of the prior wounds *as if blood-hot metal could sear what had been so violently rendered,* and he was on what he thinks was the nineteenth hole when the police arrived. Nineteenth hole, someone said. Sounds like a golf course, and everyone laughed, Janyne Watson included, everyone laughed easily at Janyne Watson and what she had to say about Walter, the man who had killed Janyne Watson's husband by stabbing him thirty-three—no, forty-eight times. Janyne Watson said Walter told her this story during their most recent visit, *three years of weekly trips out to the penitentiary and finally!* and then Janyne Watson said Amen and a host of Amens came back at her. At the time I thought it strange that someone could laugh in the middle of a story like that and then wind it up with a word that means *so be it*, but even then I saw that the thing to do in Group is what everyone else does, so I said it too, or almost said it. I moved my lips but no sound passed them: *Amen.*

So be it.

Wha—?

Shenandoah Waters jumped when I spoke, and I turned to him but didn't say anything. Behind his glasses his eyes were wide with confusion, but then he relaxed and chuckled and said, Guess I'm a little jumpy, I guess, and I nodded but still didn't speak. My mouth was filled with an ancient flavor, that last drop of pop gone viscid and metallic after hours lingering at the bottom of an open can, and even as Shenandoah Waters's window rolled down with a protesting squeal I remembered that one of the windows in the living room had been open that morning—the window that from the outside was shadowed by a boxwood hedge—and the rain had come in steadily all day and rendered a patch of white carpet a slushy gray the same color as the pearls on my mother's chest. Ahead of us a heat mirage wavered over the highway's arc of gray asphalt, next to me Shenandoah Waters exchanged a lungful of prison air for the wind-blown dust of his new condition, and then I remembered something else. I remembered touching my mother's belly. I'd just put my hand on it at first, but when nothing happened I pushed so hard a sigh was forced from her open mouth, and though what came out was, I do believe, invisible, still, I saw it, a cloud thick and pale green as a spring onion. It was nothing more than a blur, of course—everything seen through those glasses was no more frightening than a blur—but for a moment I caught a glimpse of that same cloud on the seat between me and Shenandoah Waters. When I turned I saw it was just his duffel bag. Nineteen years ago the mirage had also lasted only a moment: I'd reached a hand out to it and then, like my mother, like the apparition of water in the distance and like the hatred I'd once felt for Shenandoah Waters, it disappeared as soon as I got close.

SOME MEN CARRY jail on their backs. They hunker down, hunched over under the weight of it, their shoulders drooping, their heads dropping into their chests. Shenandoah Waters talked a lot at first, but as we got closer to town his words slacked off, his back bowed even more, eventually he fell silent, he stared at his hands, which rested a handcuff's width apart on the creases ironed into his jeans. The drive took nearly two hours, and during the ride his head sank lower and lower as his spine curved under his invisible burden. He didn't look up until we were a few blocks from my house, and then his head jerked up, he pushed his glasses up the bridge of his nose and looked out the windows, and then, with an almost audible gulp, he pushed his chin back into his chest. I thought about putting my hand on his knee then, telling him that I carried the same weight on my back: we all did. One of the things we learn in Group, one of the few things I have no trouble believing, is that no one's innocent after a crime. No one's free. And then I did put my hand on his knee, and Shenandoah Waters gulped again, and the muscles of his thigh were so taut it seemed I could feel his constricting throat under my fingers.

My parents never got married, I said. My grandma says my dad was a deadbeat, and she had plans. My mom had plans. She was working as a broker even before she got pregnant with me, and by the time—by that time she had a pretty good business, and she owned two houses in this neighborhood.

Only then did I pat his knee, remove my hand.

So no.

Shenandoah Waters rubbed his knee as if checking for an injury. No?

No, it's not the same house. My dad sold that one.

Shenandoah Waters looked again at the silvered wood of shingled roofs, at Bermuda grass and purple impatiens and the open-fan leaves of the spindly ginkgoes that had replaced the elms that succumbed to blight a few years after he'd been convicted of murder, and then he said, It was a nice house?

I guess. Kind of small I guess. A cottage really. My mom turned the attic into a second story, so we could have separate bedrooms. I tried to dam it, but the word poured out of me anyway. Ironic, huh?

Ironic?

I mean, if she'd never put in the second story, there never would've been a staircase for her to fall down.

Oh, Shenandoah Waters said. *Ironic.*

When we got to my house Shenandoah Waters opened his car door well enough; he stood up, even managed to hoist his pack onto his shoulders. Then he just stood there in the afternoon sunlight, blinking, watching me through his glasses, and I was caught for a moment by the sight of the man who had killed my mother standing on a mowed green square of suburban lawn. With his right hand, he fingered the spot over his heart where for nineteen years an ID number had been sewn into his shirts, but finding nothing there his fingers dug through the fabric into his skin. His foot scraped the dirt a little; other than that he didn't move except to blink repeatedly, whether at me or the unbarred sun I couldn't tell.

I shook my head, straightened my spine.

C'mon. You're a free man. Act like one.

For the first time his smile didn't seem forced. Your front door locked?

Yeah. Why?

Well, seeing as my house-breaking days are behind me, there's not much for me to do till you open it.

He laughed a little, and I looked at him while he laughed, and when he was done I said,

Touché.

Inside, I said: As you can see, it's way too big for one person. Too big for two really, that's why my mom rented this one out. There are four bedrooms upstairs, two bathrooms, down here there's a den, a screened-in porch, even a little maid's room off the kitchen.

You sound like you a got a bit of the broker in you too.

Must run in the family.

We walked from room to room. So, um, you got a girlfriend or anything?

I'm single.

Oh. Shenandoah Waters said, and then he cleared his throat. Look, I don't want to be a imposition.

Shen, I said. Can I call you Shen? Shen, this is the opposite of an imposition. This is a once-in-a-lifetime opportunity.

That sounds like something you heard in Group.

If it wasn't for Group we wouldn't know each other. You'd be sleeping on some cold sidewalk right now.

It's noon, Shen said. It's June.

Things change. Especially the weather.

I don't understand—Shen began, but I spoke over him.

I don't understand either, Shen, but I know that this is something we need. Both of us need this, if we're ever going to move on.

But he just blinked his eyes. I don't understand, he said again. What do we need?

We were in the kitchen when he said that. Shen had carried his bag from room to room, and now I said, You wanna put that down? It looks heavy.

He laughed a little. Disjointed words dribbled from his lips, one at a time. Oh . . . yeah . . . sure . . . I . . . He caught sight of the maid's room through an open door, and he pantomimed the fact that he was going to put his bag in there before he actually put his bag in there. When he came back I had a bottle of whiskey in my hand, the glasses already on the table. Shen looked at the bottle and then at me, and then his face broke into a grin.

Welcome home, I said. Welcome back.

I poured us each a shot and we touched glasses, but neither of us drank. Shen's hand fell to the table like a man losing an arm-wrestling match. He exchanged his drink for the car keys, which I'd tossed on the table when we came in.

Seventy-six?

I nodded.

For the first time he perked up.

No shit. I knew it, man. She's cherry. Then his smile faded again. I went to jail in '76.

That seemed to me to be beside the point, but all I said was, Last of the big Monte Carlos. Last, biggest, and best, and even before I finished Shen was shaking his head.

Naw, man. Best was '72. Half Caddy, half tank, half wolverine. Climbing into that car was about as good as climbing into pussy.

Now I put my glass down. Behind his glasses, Shen's eyes closed.

Aw man. Nineteen years. Aw *man*. When you're locked up the thought of pussy is like god, man. There was times I'd reach up outta my bunk and touch that shit like it was right there, pussy like the size of a grizzly bear waiting to eat me up. My cellie used to say, Hey everybody, Shen's having the pussy dream again. I like to kill that nigger when he do that. I mean, I don't give a shit what nobody thinks about me, but he woke me up, you know what I'm saying, and when that pussy was gone there was no getting it back until it *came* back. Nineteen years I been having that dream, and I swear to Christ that pussy got bigger every year. Big enough to open wide and swallow me whole, big enough to take me right back where I started from. Nineteen years. *Aw man.*

When he was done I said, She's yours if you want her.

She?

The car, Shen.

A new expression crossed his face, something that wasn't quite suspicion, and then Shen let go of the keys and picked up his glass and touched it to mine where it sat on the table. His eyes squinted shut as soon as the whiskey hit his throat and he slipped the thumb and index finger of his free hand under his glasses to wipe a tear from beneath tightly squeezed lids; on the table, his hand pawed the Formica, and I suddenly thought of a dog my father got me soon after I went to live with him. The dog had spent its life in a kennel, six or seven years, and when it was first set loose in the wide-open space of my father's yard it refused to run, to walk around even. It took just a few steps, wobbling like a newborn fawn, then turned and retraced its path, and then, eventually, turned again. It was months before the animal seemed to realize it was no longer in a cage, and as soon as it did it ran away and we never saw it again.

I wondered if Shenandoah Waters would realize he was free. I wondered if—*when*—he'd run away from me, but when he spoke his voice was hoarse and dry.

Aw man.

THAT NIGHT I dreamed about Shenandoah Waters. I dreamed I measured every single part of his body with a tailor's tape, chest and waist, wrists and ankles, fingers and toes even, and then I sewed him a new suit of skin, this one fresh and white, clean of tattoos and history. He grinned sheepishly when I asked about the tattoos. They used to steal his glasses, he said, wouldn't give them back until he submitted one more time. Dumb asses could draw okay but they sure couldn't spell. He held out his arm: *Jezuz*.

In the morning I knocked on the door to the maid's room before pushing it open. Shen slept through my knock, facedown on the little twin I'd bought a few weeks before he was paroled. He'd managed to undress before falling atop the sheets, and on his uncovered skin I could see more tattoos: a vine-wrapped cross on his calf, a rattlesnake's tail curled around his waist, and, on each shoulder blade, a little flightless wing. The rest of his skin was as pale and new as I'd dreamed it, save for a thin patch of hair above the label of his inside-out underwear (I could see him, glasses off, blurrily pulling them on at the sound of yesterday's reveille bell). The wings on Shen's shoulder blades flapped as he rubbed the hairs on the part of his back I was looking at, and then some prison sense must have told him he was being watched because his hand froze and his eyes sprang open. For a moment they were filled with fear and confusion, and even as he felt for his glasses on the floor I saw the two faded indentations high on his nose, and then his glasses were on his face and the confusion left his eyes, but not, immediately, the fear. He tried to smile but it came off as a grimace, the grimace of a teenaged boy who looked incapable of killing a fly, let alone a woman.

Aw, man. What'd you put in my drink?

You're out of practice. You'll get used to it.

Shen grimaced again. Maybe I should quit while I'm ahead.

I'm going to work. I thought you might like to go with me. I talked to my supervisor, he said he could probably get you something in the warehouse. You don't have anything else lined up, do you?

Well, as a matter-a fact, no.

Good. You can drive me. Better get a move on, we'll be late.

In the car he was a kid again, a cocky seventeen-year-old whose rap sheet was filled with nothing more serious than a string of B-and-E's. He tilted the seat back, rolled up his sleeve before letting his tattooed arm hang out the open window; if he could have seen the front of the car without them, I'm sure he'd've taken off his glasses. Damn, he said. Wish I still smoked. Car like this deserves a cigarette. He gunned it, and the speedometer's upward surge was matched by the gas gauge's downward spiral. Fuck you, OPEC. He looked at me. Goddamn camel jockeys took the fun outta everything. Ten hours later we were back at the kitchen table. Empty plates were pushed to one side, drinks sat between us, just pop this time, cold cans perspiring in the warm air. The workday had lasted two decades: Shen's five-o'clock shadow was tinged with gray, and the hand he ran over his lined forehead revealed a receding hairline. His prison burden weighed heavy on his back tonight, and he slouched in his chair, occasionally stealing glances at me from the corner of his eye.

Finally I said, Shoot.

Shen jumped. Huh?

What's on your mind, Shen? You haven't said two words since we left work.

Oh. It's just you said—He pointed his finger at me, pulled the trigger, and then he looked a little shocked and he put his hand on his chair, under his leg. He was silent for another moment and then he said, It's just—the house, the car, the job. It's a little much, especially on my first full day out. Don't get me wrong, man. It's not that I ain't grateful.

One of the things they say in Group—

I stopped because he was rolling his eyes.

Hear me out, okay? One of the things they say in Group is that people spend their grief. They buy a bronze casket or silver urn, they arrange to have roses put on the grave every month, every week even, every day. Okay? But other people invest it. My dad's one of those. He dropped the forty-five grand he made off my mom's house into mutual funds. He made a couple good guesses along the way, got lucky a few times, and here we are.

Shen just shrugged. Whatever.

What I'm trying to say, Shen, is that I can afford it. I'm saying it's worth it to me, whatever it costs.

But what're you buying, man? Are you trying to buy *me*?

I tried to laugh his fears away, but what could I say? The truth was I recognized his questions: I'd asked the same questions when I first went to Group, until I realized there was no answer to them: you had to learn to stop asking. I tried to explain it to him, told him I'd been doubtful too. I told him how I'd sat there dumbfounded as Raylene Cummings recounted the night Raymond Church had driven a knife into the meat of her right shoulder and then, with the knife still lodged in place, had raped her. Now, I told Shen, Raylene Cummings *paid visits out to the penitentiary* once a week. She baked Raymond Church a cake on his birthday and he knitted her loose cardigans with big wooden buttons that were easier for her to fasten with just her left hand: nerve damage had left her right arm numb and useless, and it hung from her shoulder like a wet flag on a windless day. I told Shen how Karl Grable had come home and found his wife and son *like that*. Nearly twenty years afterward he still couldn't say what *like that* meant, but every other Sunday he *took services out to the penitentiary* with Brian Dawes, the one who'd left Karl Grable's wife and son *like that*, and he'd even bought Brian Dawes a white button-down shirt and tie so he wouldn't have to sit in the Lord's cinderblock chapel in his working clothes. And then I told Shen about Lucy Ames. Like me, Lucy Ames had lost a parent. Unlike me, nine-year-old Lucy had sat in a chair and watched as George Ferguson pistol-whipped her father in an attempt to beat the location of his wife's jewelry box out of him. *Seven times he popped him*, until on the seventh time the gun went off as it struck Mr. Ames' face and the back of his head sprayed across the living room wall in a wide arc *like a rainbow where all the colors are red*. Now Lucy Ames was married to George Ferguson and *thanks to the grace of god and monthly nuptial visits out to the penitentiary* she was expecting their second child.

And, I told Shen, it wasn't like these stories convinced me of anything, but curiosity outweighed skepticism. At first I told myself I was going back because I wanted to hear more of these fascinating tales, but eventually I realized I was curious about him. I realized I wanted to meet him.

I wanted to meet the man who killed my mother.

At some point while I spoke I'd picked up my empty pop can and used my dinner knife to cut it in half, lengthwise. I didn't really register the awful squeaking the dull blade made as it sawed through two inches of aluminum until the sound was gone, and then I looked up at Shen, who stared at the cut-open can in my hands with the look of a rabbit transfixed by a pair of oncoming headlights. I tried to grin, but even as my lips curved I was bringing one half of the can to my mouth, my nostrils flared at the long-ago scent, and then I stuck my tongue against the can's exposed inner surface. The taste was obscured by memory—rain, pearls, the fleeing genie of my mother's last, forced breath—and the only way I could share that with Shen was by holding the other half out to him. I waited to see what he would do. At first he just stared at me. Then he took the can in his hands and pulled the twisted metal open like a halved fruit and raised it to his mouth. I watched his tongue flicker out and lick up the last few drops of pop. I think I was hoping he'd understand what I was trying to do because I needed him to explain it to me, but he was just as lost as I was, just as caught up. Neither of us knew what we were working towards, but in the thin clink of metal against the tabletop was the certainty that he would stick around until we'd done it.

THE CIRCLE WAS small, usually just six or seven people, sometimes as many as a dozen, every once in a while just two or three. Even with my sporadic attendance it wasn't long before I'd heard everyone's story, the pain, the loss, the grief, the inevitable victory signified by their presence in Group. Participation was voluntary, but members were strongly encouraged to share, to relate their Incident and describe the aftermath. You might recognize some of the words from some of the recovery/survivor groups, but in Group we're taught not to think of survivors or victims or perpetrators: everyone's a Person, before and after the Incident, and the only thing Group does is remind us of that fact. I managed to worm my way out of testifying for a long time but finally no one would listen to my excuses anymore and so I took my place in the center of the Circle and told them what I knew, which wasn't much. An apparent robbery, my mother's return home, a push down the stairs, a broken neck. Rigor mortis and the can of pop and then my father. I left out the glasses and the pearls and the cloud of green gas I'd pushed out of my mother's belly because that didn't seem relevant to Group, and when I'd finished telling the story Lucy Ferguson, gently rocking on her knee the eldest son of the man who had killed her father, said, Well, what does he have to say? I thought she meant my father, but she meant Shenandoah Waters, and when I told her I had no idea she said, Well then I think it's high time you found out, and Raylene Cummings said, High time is better than no time, and Janyne Watson led the chorus of Amens. The next day Lucy Ferguson picked me up when she went to visit her husband. *Out to the penitentiary.* I held George Jr. on my lap because Lucy Ferguson believed in god and she believed in Group but she didn't believe in child safety seats. Trap my baby boy in a hunk of burning metal? she cooed. How could I even think of such a thing?

I don't know what I expected to happen when I confronted my mother's killer, but I certainly wasn't prepared for the sense of disappointment I felt when he shuffled into the room. The shuffling wasn't caused by leg irons or anything so dramatic: Shenandoah Waters was simply a man who shuffled, and stooped, and squinted behind Buddy Holly glasses held together at the bridge with a rolled-up Band-Aid. His skinny frame swam inside his orange jumpsuit. His hair was cut short, parted on the side, combed over neatly. He was thirty-two years old, but he looked and acted like a teenaged refugee from some fifties sitcom, and I remember thinking that this wasn't the sort of man who should kill your mother. Shenandoah Waters's shuffling feet were loud on the concrete floor, the metal balls of his chair squeaked something awful when he pulled it away from the table to sit down, but after he'd slumped into his seat there was a long moment of silence between us, during which I heard Lucy Ferguson say, Let's show Daddy our new tooth! I considered opening lines: I wish you were dead; You're a monster; I've dreamed of this day for years. But none of these statements was true, not even the last, and in the end all I could come up with was: You're smaller than I expected. Shenandoah Waters blinked when I said that; I imagine he'd also expected something more dramatic. Behind his glasses his eyes flitted about, as if looking for something to say, and then he just said, I, um, I'm five-foot-seven. He paused. In my socks. Visiting sessions lasted an hour, and I had to wait another hour while Lucy Ferguson, after being thoroughly frisked, retired to a little tin trailer in the center of a chain-link cage in the prison yard. I held George Jr. in my lap and I silently repeated the words *my mother's killer is five-foot-seven* until Lucy Ferguson finally pushed open the trailer door and blew a kiss to her husband inside. *Five-foot-seven*, I told George Jr. *In his socks.*

AFTER THE FIRST night I offered him an upstairs bedroom but Shen said maybe he was better where he was. A pattern developed: morning coffee, work, dinner, then story time. We talked for hours every night, sometimes while drinking, sometimes cold sober. I told Shen about Group and he told me about prison. Neither of us was telling the truth, really, by which I mean that neither of us was telling the other what he really wanted to know. Every night I started from the beginning, from my first appearance at a meeting, and worked forward; and every night Shen started at the end, from his long walk out those open gates, and worked backwards, and both of our stories were bound by the same unmentioned endpoints: by my mother's death, and by our current cohabitation, and in some way these two things became conflated in my head, and, I think, in Shen's too, and our life together took on an inflection of punishment and penitence. Unbidden, he drove me to and from work, signed his paychecks over to me for rent and food, cooked and cleaned and mowed the lawn, and he did it all with the same meek acquiescence with which he'd licked the inside of the pop can I'd given him on our second evening together. Sometimes, when we'd been drinking, he'd slouch in his chair and stare at me through his glasses, and sometimes, when we'd had too much, he'd take his glasses off and his eyes would glaze over and I knew I was little more than a pale blur to him, but even though I wanted to I never reached over and put his glasses on my own nose, even though I knew he wouldn't protest if I did. In fact the only thing that ever got a rise out of him was when I asked him to come to Group.

In my six years in Group only one member had ever brought in his Person. That's what we called them in Group: People. Not murderers or rapists or muggers or thugs. By calling them People we reminded ourselves that they were as human as we were. Clay Adams had run a pawnshop downtown for forty-six years, until the day Blake Moore came in and, in Blake's own words, *went a little crazy in the head I guess.* He hadn't brought a gun, he said, *cause I was the kind of sonofabitch who'd've used it,* but relied instead on a cattle prod, which in an attempt to torture the existence of a safe out of Clay Adams he'd applied to the soles of the old man's feet again and again *till what they looked like,* Blake Moore said, *was Neapolitan ice cream, melted.* As it turned out there was no safe, and all Blake Moore got for his troubles was $5.47 from the till, a ceramic statue of two intertwined black panthers, and eight years in jail. Clay Adams had recovered the statue, and the money too, but, old and diabetic, he'd lost first his feet and eventually both legs up to the knee, *all told it took about a year and half before they stopped cutting.* He was seventy-eight years old when Blake Moore pushed him in his wheelchair into the center of the Circle and, eyes brimming with tears, presented Blake Moore with the statue he'd so coveted. He said, *I just want to thank you, Blake Moore, before god and Group, for allowing me to forgive you and forgive myself for what happened.* Blake Moore had lost the tips of the fingers on his right hand beneath a metal press—*yes ma'am, license plates*—and with the smooth soft stumps he stroked the sleek black cats on his lap. After Blake Moore's trial the police had returned the statue to Clay Adams and he'd *dashed the damned thing to the ground*, but six years in Group and a lot of super glue had all but done the trick. One of the cats was missing an ear, *but an ear ain't much*, Clay Adams said, *or a foot. Or fingers*, Blake Moore added, *not when you get right down to it. Not compared to bliss*. Not so long after that, Clay Adams died of a stroke brought on by his diabetes, and about a year later Blake Moore went back to jail, this time for stealing cars, but the general consensus was that he'd been helped by his visit to us: at least he'd chosen a line of thievery that jeopardized no one's safety but his own.

But none of this impressed Shen. He just shook his head and said:

I don't like crowds.

But that's the beauty of it. It's like the other people aren't there at all, and you can say the kinds of things you'd never say one on one, like this. I didn't look at Shen when I said that, because even though I knew what I was saying was true, I also knew that it was the problem with Group. That feeling of superhuman isolation became all of you, obscuring everything else. Shen seemed to sense this instinctively. In the end I struck a bargain with him: he could skip Group if he'd tell me something.

Like what?

My mouth watered, and I blushed and swallowed, then said, Why our house?

Shen squirmed in his chair.

I said, It was a small house, this is a prosperous neighborhood. Why ours?

Your mom, Shen said, and stopped. Your mom was on a date with this guy I knew. That's how I knew she wouldn't be home.

My mother was on a date?

Shen shrugged and refused to meet my gaze. She was twenty-six years old. Just because she had a kid didn't mean she was—He shrugged again.

We left it at that, and I went to the meeting on my own. Every week I'd ask him to join me, and every week he refused. Sometimes I demanded a piece of information in exchange for letting him off the hook, but eventually I gave up that practice because I didn't like the things he told me. I didn't like the fact that my mother had gone on a date with a man who was friendly with a house breaker, and I didn't like the fact that my mother had been humming "Afternoon Delight" when she entered her house at one in the morning, and I didn't like the fact that Shenandoah Waters called our house a slim haul—*no silver, no cash, just a couple of rings and bracelets and shit, a pair of dinner-table candlesticks that were probably tin but just in case*—and I especially didn't like the fact that it was the candlesticks my mother had tripped over. When he heard my mother come in—humming "Afternoon Delight"—Shenandoah Waters had tried hiding in the linen closet at the top of the stairs, but my mother had apparently decided to take a shower, or maybe she just wanted to dry

her hair. At any rate she went straight to the closet for a towel
without even bothering to unzip her raincoat, and when she'd
pulled open the door he'd screamed; she'd screamed; he'd
dropped his near-empty bag of booty and run and she'd run after
him, only to trip on the candlesticks and send them both sprawl-
ing down the stairs. Somewhere in the fall he'd lost his glasses and
she'd lost her life, and when he'd figured out the latter fact he'd
stumbled half blind out into the night.

I told him I didn't believe him.

Neither did the court.

Why should I believe you?

Look, the reason why I went to jail is cause if I hadn't of been
in that house your mother wouldn't've died. Everything else is
just kind of incidental. If it makes you feel better to think I
pushed your mom down the stairs, fine: I pushed your mom
down the stairs.

I suppose I liked that fact least of all.

MEAD PRITCHARD WAS the one person nobody ever talked
about in Group, Mead Pritchard and Howard Firth. Howard
Firth had served seven years for shooting Mead Pritchard in the
stomach during the course of a liquor store holdup, and when he
was released Mead Pritchard had staked out Howard Firth's front
porch for several weeks in an effort to befriend him, and then
he'd disappeared, later to be found at the bottom of Pheasant
Pond with an unopened sack of cement tied to his scarred belly.
In the absence of Mead Pritchard, Howard Firth's name never
came up, but when Mead's did people tended to say *he did what*

he had to do. I wondered if they would say that about me, but I doubted it.

I sensed my interest in Group waning after Shen finally told me how my mother died, but for some reason my interest in him seemed to grow; though I continued to go to meetings, I'd sometimes sneak out during a coffee break. I'd drive home and park down the block, and then I'd stand outside the windows spying on Shen as he watched TV with the lights off or slept with the lights on, until the night I came home and saw neither lamplight nor the TV's flickering glow. And I admit: the first emotion I felt was relief, but it was almost immediately blotted out by loss. I thought Shen had finally left me, but something, either nineteen years in prison or the few months we'd spent together, had skewed his sense of priorities. Shenandoah Waters could have gotten away if he'd wanted, but he chose to get laid first.

My first thought was that the woman in Shen's bed looked like the kind of woman who might sleep with a man even if she knew he was a paroled murderer: too tan, too plump, too trying to pretend she was still thirty-nine. When I snapped on the light she reacted calmly, lazily pulling the sheet over her body, but it took me a moment to realize Shen was calm too. He hadn't jumped when I came into the room, only laid on his back with his uncovered eyes pointed at the ceiling. I told myself it was the woman who angered me, her lack of shame, and it was her I lashed out at.

Don't you know what he did? I said to her. He killed my mother. And then I added, *Not yours.*

I clocked her reaction on her face: oh-my-god, oh-you're-joking, oh-my-god-you're-not-joking. Before I left the room I picked up Shen's glasses from the floor. I waited in the hallway, and after I heard the front door close I went back to the maid's room. Shen was still on the bed, his face still pointed at the ceiling, and I went over and sat on the edge of the little twin mattress. They hadn't gotten very far. At any rate Shen's underwear was still on, right side out this time. The bed was so narrow that my hip pressed against the thin fabric.

Can I have my glasses back.

Shen's voice was not quite flat when he spoke. There was an edge to his words, and I wondered if I should be afraid of him. But the truth is I wasn't afraid. The truth is it was hard for me to believe Shenandoah Waters had killed my mother, let alone that he could kill me.

Aloud, I said: I used to wonder if you'd saved me. If she would've married some jerk who would've beat the shit out of me. Who knows, maybe you even saved her. He could've beat her, taken everything she worked so hard for. But that was before I met you.

Can I have my glasses back.

It was only after I met you that I realized I'd been deprived of something. I'm sure I felt it before, that's why I went to Group, but it was only as I got to know you and realized you were a real person that I began to realize my mom had been a person too, although what kind of person I'd never know.

I *want* my glasses back.

You probably never saw her, did you? With your glasses, I mean. She was pretty. A lot prettier than that whore you just had in here.

He rolled over then. I don't know if he did it out of disgust or shame or if he simply didn't want to be touching me anymore, but he rolled away from me onto his stomach. But as soon as he did it he froze. The little wing on his left shoulder blade fluttered as a muscle underneath it twitched, but it became nothing more than a shadow after I put on his glasses, and my hand was a pale triangle at the end of my arm as it reached towards the shadow on his back. It seemed to me that the tattoo was colder than the rest of his skin, but that was probably just my imagination. I could feel my heart pounding in my chest as my hand slipped down the length of Shen's spine, until it came to rest on the rattlesnake's tail poking toward the thin nest of hair in the small of his back. I wondered if this is what Shen had felt when he pried open our window that night, this inexorable pull into the near future.

Shen, I said, but he didn't answer me. He didn't move either, and I squeezed onto the bed until my lips were right next to his ear. I'll trade you, I said. For your glasses.

—2000

III.

Idleness, not illness, has addled my brain. My thoughts are as slack as atrophied muscles, but with every loss comes a compensation. Strength fades; what remains is pliable, tenacious. I'm too weak to lift myself from bed, but my thoughts curve and twist into every nook and cranny of your life—and yours, and yours too. I miss the sunlight and the breeze, unmediated by glass and screen. I miss the cars, the people, movement. Birds. I miss birds. Pigeons, hawks, vultures, plastic pink flamingos. Some people say the universe has a dual nature: corporeal; conceptual. The physical world and the scrims through which we perceive it. They say what separates humanity from lesser creatures is our ability to negotiate the second aspect. I used to be one of those people. Then I decided those people were wrong. Now I realize they're just pragmatic. This is the privilege of the dying, of course: obnoxiousness and insight folded together, neither quite canceling the other out. Some people would say I've been dying all my life.

Sky Writing

My latest victim was a blonde. Though hipless as Wallis Simpson, she still found it necessary to negotiate the aisle with that sideways gait peculiar to novice flyers. You know the type. The ones who have this expression on their face, like at any moment they're going to get wedged between the seats and traffic behind them will roll up on them like the inevitable end of a Hollywood car chase. As this one crept along her eyes, shaded by delicately drooping straw-colored wings, flickered nervously between the ticket clutched to her chest and the numbers printed on the luggage rack. What is it about airplanes that makes people lose their short-term memory? I mean really. How hard can it be to remember "5D"?

Oh, I know. It's all theater. Mime without the makeup. Kabuki without the kimonos. Beckett without the black box. But even so, if this sweet young thing wanted me to stand so she could get to her precious window seat, she was going to have to ask. But she just opened the luggage rack, unzipped her carry-on, pulled out a book—*Something Something Pathology Something Anatomy*—tucked it between her skinny thighs, stowed first her bag, then her jacket, then her sweatshirt—"BC," as if we should all know what *that* stands for—and then just stood there fingering her textbook. I'm a lot of things, but patient isn't one of them. After about three seconds I jerked my head up, only to find myself confronted by skin as pink as a pink carnation.

Cheekbones like arrowheads, eyes blue enough to make the Navajo renounce turquoise. The girl was a vision, innocence itself, and against such unvarnished youth it was all I could do to stammer,

I-I'm sorry. The airline neglected to mention 5C was located in such close proximity to beauty.

I think I was as shocked as the girl by what came out of my mouth. She looked around, used one finger to scrape her face free of hair still wet from a recent shower—when, I wondered, was the last time *I'd* bathed?—and then, no longer able to deny I was addressing her, answered me in a white-trash accent compared to which Laird Swope would have sounded like a Brahmin:

Do what?

Accent undid what looks had wrought. I was working up the words to light into her when she was granted a reprieve by the flight attendant. He snapped the luggage rack shut and admonished the girl to take her seat so the plane could push back, and even as I stood to allow her by the attendant's eyes caught mine and lingered, I thought, a moment too long, and then he turned and hurried toward the front of the cabin. The girl strapped herself in and turned her whole body to stare out the window as the plane limped toward the runway, and only her whitening knuckles betrayed her when the great beast flapped its wings and took to the air. She turned from the window and stroked the cover of her textbook as though it were a small nervous animal, her open mouth sucking in air with almost as much ferocity as the three engines of the MD-11 propelling us up and over the North Atlantic.

The clunks and clanks of trolleys began to emanate from the fore and aft galleys. I glanced at my watch, looked over at my seat companion, then at my watch again, as if impatiently.

Almost . . . almost, I said. As if to myself.

Pardon? Etiquette laid its veil of safety over the fear in the girl's voice like smoke from the last cigarette of a prisoner facing a firing squad.

This—no, wait—*this* is the very moment Swissair 111 exploded off the coast of Nova Scotia. Two hundred twenty-nine dead, most of the bodies never recovered.

In fact Swissair 111 had taken off from JFK and flown for an hour and half before it broke apart; we probably hadn't reached Newport, but I was guessing from the glazed look on my companion's face that she had yet to learn to calculate relative distances. I failed to suppress my disappointment at our continued existence with a world-weary sigh.

What do you say we order a drink to celebrate the fact of our survival?

The textbook in the girl's lap featured one of those suppurated bodies crisscrossed by a red and blue roadmap of arteries and veins, which she traced with one well-manicured finger. It was hard to believe her smooth white skin and opalescent nail concealed such grisly infrastructure, and for the second time in our acquaintance my resolve wavered. But however inconsequential or esoteric, I have my task in life, and, steeling myself, I punched the call button.

Logan to Johannesburg, via Heathrow. For her sake, I could only hope my companion was en route to her European vacation, or twenty hours from now her poor little brain was going to be as shredded as the body beneath her hand.

AH, BUT FLYING *is* dangerous folly. In pursuit of the clouds men feathered themselves with aluminum and glass, carbon fiber and fiber optics, gutted their bodies with wire and plastic and gorged on kerosene and compressed air. The cockpit is their helmet, the fuselage their breastplate, their epaulets truly wings. In their armored exoskeletons they assault the heavens in order to conquer the earth. Girded with wings they have girdled the globe: yea, verily, they've cinched it in at the waist, shrunk it down to size, made it possible for the merest of mortals to skirt the horizon's portal, and for that most men lift up their hands in praise of the aviators. But not, obviously, my seat companion, who, along with an accent and enough money to afford a first-class ticket across the Atlantic, shared a loathing for airplanes almost equal to that of Laird Swope. I stress *almost*, for no one could hate flying more than Laird. He hated not just the act but the accoutrements: hated the continually deteriorating smell of the monster's innards, hated the feel of polyester against the back of his neck and every flight attendant uniform ever designed, hated tray tables and smoking restrictions and the magazine selection and the suck of air on his testicles when he flushed the pneumatic toilet, and he especially, especially in first class, hated the food.

Thank *gawd*, he always said, for the booze.

They bill at the end of the flight, is what I told the girl as I pocketed the five she gave me for her drink, a rum and cherry Coke. Don't worry your pretty little head, I'll take care of it. I beg your pardon, I added as, chagrined, she put away her college ID, my name is Francis Kaplan Pelton, but you may call me Francis.

Feather, she said, in between nervous gulps at her drink. *Fay-ther*.

A fitting name for a wingless angel. I clinked my whiskey against her cocktail.

*Hea*ther, she insisted. My name's Heather Beaumont. I'm from Texas. *Tix-us*.

I refuse to hear it. Once christened, so named. Imagine if Adam had allowed the original inhabitants of Eden a second chance. Turtles would be swans, lions mere bacilli. Feather it is, for the duration of our journey.

In answer, she glanced out the window—nothing but cloudless sky—then practically jerked her face back toward mine. She sipped, swallowed, sipped again; seemed surprised to find her glass empty. I'm going to the Velt.

There is a *d* in there, my darling, but don't let it deter you. Let us dispense with *d*'s. I—I waved my own empty glass, more to attract the flight attendant than for dramatic emphasis, but the effect was the same—am going nowhere.

She burst into laughter. Oh my god! Are folks on airplanes always this weird?

Tuesday, I suddenly remembered. I had showered last Tuesday, six days ago, in Sky Harbor. On Friday I'd given myself a fairly decent sponge bath in the Admiral's Club in Orly, and I'd just had time to wash my face in Dulles before catching the shuttle to Logan this morning. As discreetly as possible, I sniffed at my underarms. They were good—good enough anyway. At any rate, Heather seemed far too preoccupied with breathing through her mouth to notice.

Feather, I said, and was rewarded with a blush. Feather, I've spent the last year and a half on airplanes. Despite the various diversions, I said, and indicated the textbook in her lap, the monitors mounted in the seat-backs in front of us, and the round ass of the first-class flight attendant making his way up the aisle, despite all of this, flying is essentially a static experience. So I've had to invent a few games to amuse myself. To distract my somewhat floribund imagination from the fact that I and my fellow passengers are separated from death by the thinnest membrane of steel and plastic. I like to think of flying as fucking the sky in a giant condom, I practically drolled my way to the punchline, but even the roughest sex can be smoothed over with enough lubrication, don't you think? I rattled the ice in my drink.

It was a good thing that real glasses were used in first class: Heather's clutching hands would have cracked mere plastic.

Well, I could get into that, she said after a moment. I don't know about you but I could sure use more *lubrication* right about now.

Our flight attendant, him of the once-overs and double-takes and well-rounded ass, was called Gavin, and he sighed dramatically when, finally, he responded to my call button. He puckered his lips and forced a gush of breath from his mouth as though he were attempting to blow the hair out of his eyes, a gesture made all the more symbolic by the slick mousse that held his close-cropped bristles off his high forehead.

How may I help you? he panted, *sir*.

I held out my glass. Another, I said. *And*, I added, since you seem so pressed for time, one in reserve.

Gavin opened his mouth, closed it without speaking. He took my glass from me and held it under his nose. Then he fished in the pocket of his apron until he came up with a tiny bottle of Maker's Mark, which he presented to me with a flourish.

And also for my friend, I said, handing him Heather's glass. Rum and—

Cherry Coke. The naive smile Heather gave Gavin was completely misdirected, as was the five she gave me, but Gavin chose not to comment on either phenomenon.

So—I kept one eye on Gavin's retreating form—B is for Boston, I presume.

Heather crunched a piece of ice between her jaws. Do what?

C is for College?

Oh. Heather stroked the phantom letters on her chest in a gesture that would have made a straight boy cry. Statistically speaking, she had a fifty percent chance of being raped, but each of those breasts raised the odds another twenty-five percent, and of course she was a blonde. I felt another twinge of pity but didn't let it hold me back.

I go to Bates, she said. In Maine. But the airport in Bangor—*banger*, she said, the way a hoodlum might have said *fuck her*—doesn't fly direct to anywhere except Boston. I have to spend like a day and a *half* on airplanes.

Is *that* all? I handed her the drink Gavin had brought while she'd been talking. Attitude or no, he was almost as nice to look at head-on as he was from the rear, and the wry, sly smile that played on his face made him all the more intriguing. Forget about a bath, I thought. When was the last time I'd gotten *laid*? Well, I could probably figure that one out to the day as well, if I cared to.

Y'all are gonna get me *so* plastered, Heather giggled, and I realized her *you all* lumped me and Gavin together: the fags. Perhaps she wasn't as naive as I'd assumed. She sipped at her second drink, using the cocktail stirrer as a straw. What about you?

I can assure you I have every intention of getting plastered.

I meant, like, do you live in Boston?

I faked a shudder.

Although I have it on good faith that several million people reside in the Boston vicinity, I'm not sure anyone actually *lives* there.

Oh. When I wasn't forthcoming: Were you there on business? Or something? Vacation?

Neither.

Heather shrugged. So what brought you to Boston?

I believe it was a McDonnell Douglas Super 80.

Do what?

A small twinjet whose engines are mounted to the rear fuselage. Passengers in the back of the cabin, besides being subjected to a nauseating combination of kitchen and bathroom aromas, have to endure a shockingly loud roar for the duration of their journey.

If nothing else, alcohol made Heather sassy. Why, I bet you've never flown *steerage* in your life.

Did you learn that word from *Titanic*? Heather blushed again.

It might surprise you to find out I've spent a significant amount of time loitering in the back of airplanes, and in kitchens for that matter, and bathrooms—

There was a bump then, a tiny one, but Heather yelped and grabbed my arm. Her fingernails cut into my wrist so deeply I almost yelled as well. It was a moment before she released me, and then she picked up her glass and sucked a piece of ice into her mouth.

I don't really like thinking about the engines and all that. She patted the textbook in her lap. I'm pre-med. I prefer internal mechanics. She stroked the textbook nervously.

My dear, if that textbook were not *exactly where it is*, your fingers could be indicted for lewd behavior. Heather's hand flew from her lap to her mouth, and her pale cheeks reddened yet again. But perhaps you can be the one to help me, I went on, taking the textbook from her lap and tucking its grisly image in the magazine pocket in front of her. Tell me: how, exactly, does one die of asphyxiation?

For a moment Heather froze. Then she smiled uncertainly. You're, um, serious?

I nodded.

You mean, like, how do you actually *die*?

I nodded again.

Heather's nervous hands fluttered between her chest and her lap, then reached for her glass. Her fingers curled around the crystal cylinder as though she were choking it. I guess we're, um, we're talking about mechanical obstruction?

Let's say a tie. I looked down at my chest. Let's say, for the sake of argument, an Hermès tie.

Do what? She reached for her textbook, let a single finger sit on its edge as though she could absorb its contents through osmosis. Okay, she said, leaning back in her seat. So the, um, the tie squeezes the windpipe but it doesn't actually close it. What usually happens is that the root of your tongue is pushed up and it blocks your air intake. She smiled slightly, went on in a more confident tone. At the same time the jugular and the other veins that drain the cranial cavity *are* blocked, even though the heart still manages to push a little arterial blood past the constriction. That's why people who've been hung get those big puffy faces.

Big puffy *blue* faces.

Well, yeah, they go cyanotic. Oxygenated blood is red, well, it's maroon really, but deoxygenated blood is bluish, and as carbon dioxide builds up it gets even darker. As she spoke I pretended to fiddle with the knot of my tie, and Heather stared at my fingers as they pushed it a little tighter around my neck. And so anyway, hypercarbia actually makes you nervous. I mean, I'm sure anyone would be nervous if they were choking to death—with an effort she tore her eyes from my throat—but a buildup of carbon dioxide in the blood causes anxiety, and so the victim tends to flail around a lot. But at the same time the cerebral cortex, which controls speech and, like, what we would call thinking—*thankin*—the cerebral cortex begins to function at progressively deteriorating levels of performance, and a lot of people who've nearly choked to death say that after a minute or two they actually forget what's wrong even as they're completely freaking out. Her clutching fingers found the strap of her seatbelt then, pulled it tight around her waist. And then, you know, if the blocked passage isn't opened critical mass is reached. Cells die, the heart rate becomes erratic, the victim loses consciousness. The heart stops beating and then, you know, that's usually it.

As a matter of fact, I *do* know, I said, unbuckling my own seatbelt. A bravura performance. As Laird Swope himself might have put it, you could have shit the shit yourself. Now, if you will excuse me, I must retch my eggs. Er, stretch my legs. I nodded towards the bulkhead. I'm sure you understand.

Just outside the door to the lavatory I felt a hand on my shoulder. It was Gavin. He wore the look of a gossip just dying to share his latest tidbit, but when I didn't return his smile it faded from his pale, pretty cheeks. He took his hand from my shoulder and attempted, without much success, to inject an officious note into his voice.

I've seen you before.

The perils of fame.

You're about as famous as my—He took a breath. I've seen you on this flight before.

Gavin. Were you about to make an improper reference to a part of your anatomy?

Gavin's reddening cheeks gave him away. In fact, I believe you were on this plane last Tuesday, Mr. Pelton.

I see your ability to remember faces is matched only by your facility with a passenger manifest.

I should inform you, Mr. Pelton—

Please. Call me Francis.

I should inform you, Mr. Francis Pelton, that in addition to getting you drunk I am also expected to be aware of any irregularities that might affect the integrity of this aircraft.

Integrity isn't the word I would have chosen, but if you're so concerned perhaps you'd like to frisk me for weapons. I tapped the door to the lavatory.

The authoritarian pose proved too much for him, and Gavin looked ready to go all black girl until I cut him off with a stern shake of my head.

Now now, Gavin. To the best of my knowledge a predilection for certain sky lanes is indicative of little more than weakness of character on my part. So if you will excuse me, I have an urgent need to rid my body of some of the alcohol with which you have so professionally plied me. I opened the door. Oh, and Gavin? I think my seat companion could use another of her rum and cherry colas. And while you're at it—

Why don't I just leave the cart, Gavin said, and spun on his heel before I could close the door in his face.

A GOOD GIRL, that Heather Beaumont. As soon as I returned to my seat she asked the question she had been primed to ask.

Who's Laird?

Would you say that again, please.

Who's Laird?

Just the second word, please.

Laird?

It's been so long since I've heard anyone say it properly. Most people usually spit it out in a single syllable, *Lard*, either dropping the terminal *d* or else over-aspirating it, so the word comes out

Lar-duh. But you, my dear Feather, have diphthonged it into the appropriate two fully twanged syllables. *Lay-ered*. Like a cake, or a narrative, or a bad eighties haircut. Thank you.

You're welcome? She indicated our full glasses. Gavin came by. I think he likes you.

Why do you think that?

Heather leaned close to me and held up her drink. He said to tell Francis that these were on him, she whispered, and then she sat back and picked a piece of ice out of her glass with her fingers and crunched it between her teeth. I am *way* too drunk to make heads or tails out of whatever it was you just said.

Do you know, Feather Beaumont, when you crunch your ice like that you remind me of—

Elizabeth Taylor in *Who's Afraid of Virginia Woolf?* Jesus, do all gays watch the same movies? And enough with the Feather business already. She looked at her watch then, and her lips moved as she ticked off her fingers to account for the time difference. Six hours till London? It feels like we should be there already.

Only one thing can smooth our journey. I held up my drink.

Oh, what the hell. Heather touched her glass to mine, and we drank. When both our glasses had returned to their pull-out slots in the armrest between us, she said, Laird.

I nodded. Laird Swope was, until nineteen months ago, my lover. Nineteen months and change, as he might have put it. I waited until she was looking, then adjusted the knot of my tie. Alas, he is no longer with us.

Heather's eyelids, so pale they seemed nearly translucent,

dropped over the blue pools of her irises. When they were covered it was hard to believe her eyes had been as luminescent as one remembered, but when, a moment later, her lids lifted, they seemed if anything even more perfect.

Heather Beaumont said, Oh.

He was also my benefactor, and the reason why I am able to travel in such luxury.

I knew somebody in high school had a cousin named Laird. But I never heard me of a name like Swope.

Laird said it was quite common where he came from, although if you asked him where that was he would only wave his hand and say, Way out way-ust.

Heather laughed. I'm a *frayed* knot, she said, and it took me a moment to realize she'd said *I'm afraid not*. What you did was more Appalachian hillbilly than cowboy. It sounds like the past tense.

Way-ust?

Swope. Swoop, swope, had swoped. She stretched her hands as wide as the cabin's curved walls permitted and pantomimed a dive-bombing eagle. The bird swope out of the sky on its helpless prey.

It was a bit like that, yes.

Heather dropped her arms. Where is that cute little Gavin? I think we both need some more lubrication. She smacked her call button like the ass of a stubborn mule. Now then. Laird. *Luh-hay-erd*. What was he like?

Her eyes were trained full on me. When she'd smacked the call button she'd also hit the reading lamp's switch, and against its focused beam her pupils contracted until the blue of her eyes seemed nearly solid. Their color was that of the evening sky now, visible in the window beyond her shoulder.

Hmmm, I pretended to ponder. How best to characterize my dead lover? Well, once, at a dinner with a group of publishing types—writers, editors, agents, real drunks and drips—Laird refused to engage with any of them. He simply drank whiskey after whiskey and flirted with one particularly attractive waiter all night long and then, just as dessert was being ordered, got up and left the table. He returned about fifteen minutes later—with, I might add, his shirt still untucked—and all he had to say was, Now that adds a whole new meaning to the phrase *soup to nuts*.

When I'd finished Heather used her hand to push her jaw closed. It was hard to tell if she was genuinely shocked or simply giving in to drunken affectation. She seemed about to say something when, from a place that seemed very far away, a voice sang out, Dinner! and our tray tables clattered down atop our knees. Gavin practically dropped our plates on them, along with a half dozen miniature whiskeys and rums and a few cans of Cherry Coke. You'd better make these last, you two. I have *six* other people to serve, and I cannot be rushing back here every other minute.

You two. In Heather's mind I belonged to Gavin, in Gavin's to Heather. Neither of them seemed to realize that I belonged to one person only. He'd spent a fortune on me, after all, and I had the bank account to prove it.

NORMALLY BY THE time dinner was served my seat companion would have asked to move. As first class was often full, there was always an interesting negotiation when he or she had to decide which was worse: six more hours with me, or six hours in steerage. But Heather opted out of this scenario by going to sleep just before Gavin came around with dessert. I asked her if she would like my pudding, and when she didn't answer I turned and saw her pink profile smushed against the window's glass.

Looks like Miss Pretty Prairie had herself a bit too much moonshine.

I waved Gavin away without looking at him. Heather's mouth hung open; her right hand still held on to her fork. Precipitation at 39,000 feet beaded the window, and I considered moving her cheek off the cold glass but then decided not to wake her. Instead I pried the phone from its hermetic slot, swiped my credit card, dialed a number I knew by heart. After a relatively short journey through an electronic maze, Tilda came on the line and asked how she could service me. Once, on the red-eye transatlantic Virgin, I'd had the entire first class cabin to myself and I'd called a phone-sex line based in London; the man who took my call—Kirk or Kurt, between the staticky connection and his accent I could never quite make it out—had answered the phone in the same way.

Now I told Tilda, I'd like to book a seat on the 10:30 Conk to JFK.

Of course, sir. When would you like to travel?

Ten-thirty.

Tomorrow morning. Of course, sir. Let me just confirm

availability and . . . There was a bit of line noise and I couldn't make out what she said.

Come again, Tilda? These airplane phones aren't what they should be.

You're on a plane now, sir?

I'm due in at Heathrow in just over five hours.

And you'd like a seat on the 10:30 Conk to JFK? The Concorde, sir?

I know, I know, a four-hour layover. But it is the earliest flight, isn't it?

That would be correct, sir.

A moment later Tilda had ascertained that there was a seat on the 10:30 flight—as if BA could ever fill up that money pit, the poor bastards—and it could be mine for a mere thirty-five hundred pounds. When we'd concluded our business I swiped my card again and dialed another number. Shirley was the good lady who took my call, and she was only too pleased to put me on the 10 A.M. flight out of JFK to MBJ.

As soon as I hung up the phone Heather spoke.

Where's MBJ? Her accent seemed even more thick in her sleepy voice: *Wayers Em Bee Jay?*

She had a bright red stain on her right cheek that she was rubbing lightly, and the hair on that side of her head was slightly wrinkled, like fabric. Her beautiful bleary eyes looked all of ten years old.

Montego Bay, I said. Jamaica.

Going to the beach? Her tone suggested she didn't expect an affirmative answer.

The ten o'clock is the only nonstop between JFK and MBJ. Well, they put down at MIA, but you don't have to get off the plane if you don't want to. Miami, I added, before she had to ask.

I thought your, um, Concorde flight doesn't leave London till 10:30?

Supersonic transport, my dear. Leave Heathrow at 10:30 A.M., arrive JFK at 9, before you even left.

Heather reached for her glass then, then put it back down and rubbed the side of her face. I reached a hand towards her cheek, then thought better of it and pretended I was just pointing towards the window.

Did the cold give you a headache?

Do what? Oh. Heather grimaced. No, I'm pretty sure it was the rum. She nodded at the phone. So, uh, what's up with that? You just decided you didn't want to go to Johannesburg?

Laird used to say that. *Do what.* It sounded different when he said it, *dyew whut*, like the plop-plop of two horse turds landing on asphalt. But coming from you it sounds positively graceful.

Heather drawled her drawl out even further: *Do whaaat?*

I was never going to Johannesburg.

Do wha—She stopped herself, then just looked at me for a moment. I'm going to the Velt. She swallowed, attempted to spit out the *d*. The Vel-dut.

I *was* en route to JNB, but I never I had any intention of going to Johannesburg, or even leaving the airport by any other route than the air. From JNB I was going to SYD and then I planned to hop up to SIN. Sydney, I explained. Singapore. At Singapore I was going to play a game I like to call the thousand-mile hurdles.

I was going to jump from one capital to another, either Phnom Penh to Vientiane to Hanoi and on up the coast of Southeast Asia to Tokyo and across the Pacific to LAX, or else I would have taken the westbound route through Bangkok, Rangoon, Dhaka, Delhi, Islamabad, avoiding Kabul, Tehran, and Baghdad for practical reasons, and attempting to make it all the way to Amman or Beirut or possibly even Ankara, then hopscotching my way through the Balkans before heading on to Rome and back to JFK.

Heather contemplated her various responses for a long time, and in the end chose the practical route. Why'd you change your mind?

You mean, why am I deplaning at Heathrow and heading back to the States?

Um, yeah?

No offense to you, I said, and nodded at Gavin, who from the smell of things was baking chocolate chip cookies in the galley. Certain elements of this particular flight are a little too familiar, which means that it has already failed in its mission.

Its mission?

To be strange. To be new. To be singular. An airplane journey, I said, should be completely unconnected to past, present, and future. When Heather still looked at me blankly I said, Our friend Gavin? He reminds me too much of a certain waiter.

Heather looked at Gavin as he flitted back and forth between the bays of the galley. He was wearing a starched white apron smartly knotted at the waist; though unadorned, on Gavin the apron still managed to project the idea of ruffles. Now Heather cleared her throat and sipped at her drink and cleared her throat again, and then she said, What did you do? While he was away, I mean. Laird, I mean. What did you do while Laird was with the waiter?

Oh, you silly girl. I *was* the waiter.

Heather started to rise, then fell back when her seatbelt caught her at the waist. She unfastened it, rose again, then just stood there, swaying gently with the plane's slight bounce. Her face had paled again, and seemed to have acquired a greenish tint.

I have to use the restroom, she announced, her voice so loud that everyone in first class turned and looked at her.

I stood up to let her by. Good luck, I said. Hold on to the headrests to steady yourself, or you'll never make it.

Almost as soon as Heather had disappeared into the lavatory, Gavin came out of the galley and walked purposefully towards me. Without bothering to ask, he squeezed past me and sat down in Heather's seat, practically rubbing his ass in my face in the process.

Shame on you. You'd think this was a frat house party, the way you and that girl are putting them away. I shrugged, and Gavin said, She told me when she boarded that this was her first flight ever, and now she'll be lucky if she even remembers it.

She did not tell you that. She flew to Logan from Bangor, Maine. She lives in Texas. I bet she flies home every weekend so her momma's maid can do her laundry.

That little girl is up there puking her guts out.

Better than crying her eyes out.

Gavin peered at me. What do you mean? Are you tormenting *her* too?

Too? I repeated. As in also? As in you? Gavin pursed his lips but didn't elaborate. What I mean, I said, is that this might or might not be her first time in an airplane, but she's definitely terrified of them. If she wasn't vomiting from drinking too much, she'd be vomiting from fear.

Gavin glanced toward the front of the cabin then, and I saw Heather emerging from the lavatory. Like most people her age, the experience of vomiting up her liquor seemed to have refreshed her, and she walked more steadily down the aisle.

Gavin stood up. You have an answer for everything don't you, Francis? He pushed past me. But none of them are straight.

Heather had come up behind Gavin, and she looked uncertainly between the two of us.

I'm not going to touch that line with a ten-inch pole, Gavin. But if you'd be so kind as to bring me and my companion a couple of stomach-soothing ginger ales, we'd both appreciate it.

Heather waited until she was back in her seat before speaking. So how long were you two together? She kept her voice steady, and the determination in her tone impressed me: she had decided to rise to the occasion.

About five minutes, I said.

I *meant*—Heather glanced at Gavin—you and Laird.

I know what you meant, and five minutes is about as accurate as any other measurement. She frowned with the dissatisfaction of the literal-minded, so I said, All told, I'd say we fucked around for about three months.

That's it?

Heather, my dear, my fate was sealed the day I met Laird. Everything else, as he himself liked to say, was just gravy.

But how did you—She tried to stop herself, but curiosity got the better of her manners. How'd you get his money?

How does one get money? He left it to me. In fact he converted it into cash first, and he secreted it in various bank accounts around the world, and he left the access codes inside a Gideon Bible that had somehow found its way to the bedside table of the Hotel InterContinental in Melbourne, and while I was on my way to pick them up—he had asked me to run what he called a business errand—he hung himself. With the aforementioned Hermès tie. Don't worry, dear, this is a Gene Meyer. There was a will too, which codified everything and protected me from lawsuits on the part of all those poor relations, but possession, at any rate, is nine-tenths of the law. The money was mine, whether I wanted it or not. Do you want to know how much?

No, Heather said, a little too quickly, and then she said, Yes.

I told her.

This time there was no doubt in my mind that Heather's reaction was genuine. She stared at me for several moments, and something propelled me to add the final detail. Did I mention he videotaped it?

His . . . will?

His . . . death.

Oh my god, she nearly spat. The man was a freak. He was *evil*.

I patted her on the knee, but she wasn't finished yet. But, but . . . She turned to the window and stared at the darkened sky for nearly a minute before she turned back to me. But you loved him. Didn't you?

Heather, I was twenty-nine years old and I was nowhere. Ten years of auditions had landed me nothing more than a series of jobs waiting tables, and Laird Swope was a handsome man whose crotch turned out to be even more loaded than his wallet. If you don't already have an understanding of the values of these things, then—

Heather cut me off. I may not know about big dicks, Mr. Rich Fag Who Flirts With Flight Attendants, but I do know about money. My daddy's a *proctologist*. He was born in a dirt-floor shack and now he's got the biggest rear-end clinic on the Gulf. For Christmas last year he made pens that said, "Your shit is my bread and butter." Out of *gold*. A giggle interrupted her encomium. But then he was too embarrassed to give them to his patients, so he just gave them to the family.

Heather, I said firmly. When I used the word *loaded*, I wasn't referring to *size*.

Heather's eyes held mine a moment, comprehension almost but not quite entering them. I looked up to see Gavin making his way down the aisle, his head shaking back and forth. He smelled of some kind of soap and, ever so faintly, molasses.

There's a problem child on every flight, and you're mine.

He spoke to Heather but looked at me, and I was looking back at him and so was quite surprised when Heather practically fell into my lap. She was leaning over me in a manner that afforded Gavin the best possible view of her cleavage. Even though she knew the impulse was out of place, she'd not yet learned any other way to address the situation at hand.

Gavin, she said, fluttering her eyelashes. You've been so good to us that me and Mr. Pelton here would like to buy you a drink.

Alas, Gavin said, being a flight attendant is a bit like being a police officer. No drinking on the job, no matter how attractive the, um, buyer might be. He looked at me when he said *buyer*, and I just shrugged. Then, addressing Heather with mock sternness: I have to get back to my dishes, but I warn you, if I have to come back here one more time I'm turning off the tap.

Heather still lay in my lap. With some twisting, she managed to look up at me. Her cheeks were flushed, her eyes bright. Ah, Francis, she said. I feel like I've known you all your life.

But, my dear, you have. My life began when this plane took off and it shall end when it lands—only to begin anew when the next plane takes to the sky.

The Conk, Heather said, giggling a little, and then her voice sobered. I don't get it. I mean, you *live* on airplanes?

For want of a better term, yes, I live on airplanes.

But why?

Oh, I don't know. Something about the feeling of freedom that attaches to the possibility of imminent death. Memento mori, carpe diem, blah blah blah. Heather continued to look up at me with the truly naive gaze of someone who actually doesn't know what she wants to know, and I shrugged. I suppose airplanes were all he left me.

In his will?

Laird left me money in his will. He left me a whole lot of money, but only a few ways to spend it.

He wanted you to buy—Heather broke off. She shook her head; then, grimacing, stopped that too. Please, she said. I'm a young drunk redneck from the Gulf Coast of Texas. 'Splain it to me in words I can understand.

Laird was afraid of flying.

Laird . . . was afraid . . . of flying?

Laird was one of life's great capitalists. He bought and sold agricultural futures. He moved in the margin between people's need for food and the possibility that that food would actually come into existence by a specified time, and he spent the vast amounts of money he earned buying up anything he wanted, including me. The entire enterprise was based on a kind of faith: that the rain would fall but not so much the fields would flood, that the harvest would be plentiful, but the markets wouldn't glut, that an elevator fire in Kenosha, Kansas, wouldn't burn up the wheat he'd bought before it had even been planted. But despite all these purely imaginary transactions, Laird refused to believe that four thousand tons of aluminum, glass, fuel, and flesh could lift up off the ground and stay there.

When I had finished speaking Heather opened and closed her pretty blue eyes three times. The movement was lethargic but deliberate, registering the transitions between her reactions to my words. Confusion—*blink*—incredulity—*blink*—contempt—*blink*—pity.

Blink.

I just realized something.

And what is that?

I'm not scared no more. She raised her voice. I may be a hick but I'm not like Laird. And I'm not like *you* either.

Despite myself, I laid my hand on her cheek. It was cool to the touch, but even as I glanced out the darkened window my mind flashed on the bones and veins beneath Heather's smooth lotioned skin, and with as much sincerity as I could muster I said, I hope that you never do become like me.

Heather Beaumont had learned some things, but there were others she refused to know. Gently but firmly, she turned her cheek from my hand. She seemed to be casting about for something to say, but the plane chose that moment to interrupt her: the video monitors flickered into life. The in-flight entertainment was starting. Without sitting up, Heather attempted to focus on the screen in front of us. She stared at it intently with slightly glazed eyes, as if waiting for something to appear, and then her eyelids fluttered shut and her chin fell on her chest and she began to snore quietly. She was nineteen years old and she had had six or seven cocktails in the space of about three hours and she had her head on the lap of a raving lunatic: what other escape did she have besides sleep?

The lights in the cabin dimmed. Scattered ratchetings marked the recline of seat-backs and the raising of footrests. The engine's efforts produced a wall of white noise over which the only sound was an occasional thump or tinkle from the galley: Gavin, putting away the dinner dishes and making sure everything was ready for breakfast, a foreshortened night away. He walked back and forth between the central and side bays of the galley in his apron, and each time he did he glanced back into the cabin. When he caught my eye he smiled; I smiled back. He mimed drinking; I shook my head. He pretended to comb long blond hair out of his eyes, and I placed folded hands against the side of my cheek, and then I pointed down to Heather's head in my lap. Once again he mimed the act of drinking, but this time he held up two imaginary glasses, and then he motioned for me to join him in the galley.

Before I got up I took the money Heather had given me for her first two drinks and placed it inside the front cover of her textbook. On the flyleaf was a fat arrow-pierced heart enclosing the initials H.B. and D.P. Heather's sleeping face was smooth and untroubled, free of the anxious lines that a conversation with me had temporarily drawn there. I eased out from beneath her. Her head was surprisingly heavy, a literal refutation, if one were still needed, to the idea she was some kind of airhead. Would that I were D.P., I thought as I stood up, Heather's swain rather than her jaded interrogator, tormenting her with tales of the city for no other reason than that I was bored.

In front of the cabin something popped loudly, and a small bolt of fear ran through my heart. I glanced down at Heather one last time and smiled at this funny bond between us. But it was just Gavin, opening a bottle of champagne.

He'd already filled two glasses by the time I made it up front, and he held one out to me as I ducked through the stiff curtain that shielded the galley from the aisle. He'd taken off his apron, and his navy-blue tailored uniform, though flimsy polyester, was still sexy in the way that all uniforms are sexy. He was smiling. He said, A part of me would like to throw this drink in your face for being such a pain in my ass, but . . . He let his words trail off.

But a part of you wants me to be even more of a pain in your ass.

We sipped at our champagne, and then he looked at his watch. Chances are it'll be a good two hours before anyone buzzes.

I thought I was the one who was supposed to be drunken and forward.

He shrugged. They can't exactly fire me till we land, can they? Besides, I'm tired of flying all the time.

Oh Gavin. So am I.

Before he could ask about that I kissed him, and that was all we did, but we did it for a long time. When we finally broke apart I reached a hand into the breast pocket of my jacket, and Gavin's eyes went wide.

Are you getting what I think you're—He stopped when he saw what I'd pulled from my pocket: a checkbook. I put it on the counter next to my champagne glass, and then I reached back in my pocket for a little pillbox and put it on the counter as well, and then, looking Gavin directly in the eye, I unbuckled my belt.

I'd like to give you something. An old flame gave it to me, and I think it's time I passed it on.

Gavin's eyes flashed between my checkbook, my pillbox, my opened belt.

What? His eyes cleared. Oh. He took a little step back from me, caught himself with a nervous chuckle. So, he said, and shrugged. Over his shoulder a window revealed the first sprinkle of stars, a few yellow pinpricks above bands of deep blue and orange. The idea of land seemed like a dream from someone else's life. So, Gavin said again, and that was all.

Manhattan looks like a kipper as you leave it, curling in the sun. The rocks off the frothy coast of Reykjavík look like peppercorns in cream sauce as you approach, and then, as you descend, the blue of the water emerges and they look like the last crumbs of coffee cake on a Hepplewhite plate. And once I remember, though I can't remember where, I flew over a place where the view was all rolling hills. The trees studding them were leafless, from that altitude nothing more than brown pins poking from a cushion's surface, and at their bases an old snowfall whitened the ground. It was winter on earth. The scene made me think of a bolt of rumpled burlap laid over something pristine and white, and for a moment I wondered what might lie under that cover, a pale body, a marble frieze, perhaps simply another layer of cloth, and then I'd remembered that I wasn't actually looking at burlap but at trees and snow and hilly terrain, and then the airbrakes came on with a roar, the plane decelerated, a flight attendant, not Gavin, began to announce connecting flights: Ibiza, Edinburgh, Moscow, Riga, and points north. Looking out the window over Gavin's shoulder, I remembered the words and imagined a crystalline plain merging infinitesimally into the frozen sky.

Francis?

I started slightly, looked at Gavin, at the items on the counter, then refastened my belt. Gavin made no move to stop me.

So, he said. Why *do* you spend so much time on airplanes? He smiled uncertainly. Where're you going anyway?

It wasn't the kind of question I normally answered, so I was a little surprised when I heard myself saying, Points north. I shook my head, returned Gavin's uncertain smile. I tucked my checkbook and pillbox back in my jacket. Though I might fly forever, some things *would* stop with me. Points north, I said again, louder. That has a nice air to it, don't you think?

—2004

IV.

I've always been drawn to the shape of things. The shell. Tree trunks, the swell of a calf beneath a skirt. Pediments, the tube of a bicycle tire. I like outlines, edges, the mystery of cloister. I see no difference between a man's chest and a cupboard: both hide something, and I've never been able to resist filling them with lies. There are times when the inside shows itself on the outside—ribs under skin, the shadow of dishes in glass-fronted cabinetry—but most closed things like to keep their secrets. Not what's in there, nor how it got there, but why. Why is always the real mystery; what is just the thing we use to conceal that fact from ourselves. But illness has changed the nature of my vision. No, not illness—I've been sick for a long time. Dying. The indolence of death. That's what's changed me. As I lie here and look out the window, it's as if an angel is frittering away the time until she comes for me with the idle gossip of the omniscient. See that girl, the angel whispers in my ear, the one in the striped socks walking past the church? She cheated on her geography final. And that other, with the hennaed hair? Her favorite thing to do is immerse her fingers in her collie's mane. Her collie's name is Elfir. Elfir is rifle *spelled backwards, but the girl with the hennaed hair doesn't know that. She thinks it has a magical Nordic sound,* elf *crossed with* Fafnir. *The girl's name is Christina, and she'll be dead in sixty-two years, but she doesn't know that either, and won't until she's dead.*

The Law of Diminishing Returns

Someone told me they were more careful in England. He said they were more careful in Europe actually, because of all the wars. He said as a result of centuries of conflict they had less to spare over there, less to waste, and so, dutifully, but not, like the environmentalists in the States, piously, they collected their cans and plastic and paper, their dead batteries, bald tires, and scrap metal and turned it all in for recycling, they built energy-efficient appliances, took shorter showers, swaddled their children in cloth rather than disposable diapers. On account of the wars? I remember asking. They bombed the *shit* out of that place, my informant told me. Trenches, he said. Mines. Mustard gas. It all had its effect, and they're still feeling it today. Blood, he said. Blood is a poison. On some battlefields it was years before anything would grow. He said they were more careful in Europe but I had to settle, when I left, for England—the language thing—and I guess I just hoped that the English would follow the European example because I liked the idea of living among a careful people: I liked not just the idea of frugality but return, reuse, of, to put it bluntly, second chances, and it seemed at first that England, that London, where I settled, did offer that. Within a week I had a flat in a terrace house, in Bethnal Green admittedly, but it was cheap and clean, two large barren rooms with a view over my downstairs neighbor's vegetable garden, I had an umbrella, a Travelcard, an adapter cable for my computer, a phone number even, and I had

Derek. That's *my* name, I said, when he told me his. It wasn't my
name, but I would have used the line no matter what his had
been. I was a new man in a new country and I had decided that a
new name—not a new name, but a borrowed name, a recycled
one—suited the occasion, if only for a night. Your name's Derek?
he said, fancy that, and then he grinned and he said, Fancy a walk
in the park, Derek? I thought he was joking, and brought him
instead to my place—I'd gone, on a Sunday night, and on the
advice of a gay guide I'd bought, to a loud little club just down
Mile End Road—and in the morning I woke up with a large
bruise on my tailbone because I had blankets but no bed. No bed
and no Derek: he'd slipped out in the middle of the night, leaving
only the bruise and a note next to the phone. *I took the liberty of
taking your number,* he wrote. *You're a sound sleeper.* He had, in
fact, peeled off the tiny sticker affixed to the phone that BT had
provided me, and thus he didn't just take my number, he deprived
me of the ability to give it to anyone else, because I hadn't yet
memorized it. I think that's how he got me. The sex had been
great but it had also just been sex; it was the peculiar piracy of
peeling off a sticky phone label and pocketing it, so odd, so deter-
mined in securing its goal, that led me to believe Derek felt
something more than mere lust for me. At that time I believed
emotion flowed from motion, from action, that love emanated
from routine—sex, shared meals, shopping for Christmas pres-
ents—and it seemed to me that Derek's little theft was the first
step in such a routine. Now it seems to me that I was thinking
about love as if it were some kind of byproduct. Love is like trash:
it's not something you hoard, merely something you don't waste,

like heat, or water, or paper. Or words, for that matter, because what's more recycled than the language of love? The language of hate, perhaps, or the language of disinterest: Let's be friends. Which is what Derek said when he called a few days later. He said, Let's be friends, shall we? and I assented innocuously, because I was trying to think of a way to ask him what number he'd just dialed. I never did, and as a result didn't know what my phone number was until the bill came three weeks later, by which point Derek had called several more times, always during the day, and once or twice a week he stopped by on his way home from work. In the meantime I acquired a bed, a sofa, a table and two chairs, enough dishes to feed as many as four people at the same time, and my flat absorbed these new acquisitions and still somehow seemed empty, and so, as an exercise, I typed up every single thing in the flat that wasn't attached to it by nails or glue, starting with myself and ending with three loose paper clips I found in the bottom of my computer case, and the entire list, single-spaced, a single entry per line, stretched to seven pages. I felt a little better then, and reminded myself how deceptive appearances can be. The list went with me on my first trip to the local recycling center, but the pages I left there were just as quickly replaced by an office supply store I'd found that sold unbleached stock made from 100% post-consumer waste. I had, as they say, gotten my break, and I was working on a screenplay, and also several treatments, and the amount of paper I went through was unconscionable. I wrote at home, all day, every day; the words barely trickled out of me but even so the pages seemed to flow from my printer, the spool of fax paper spewed forth a cataract of queries and comments and suggestions for cutting that seemed to require twice as much new material to fill the gap, and the stacks of paper I took regularly to the recycling center were embarrassingly large. I'd been . . . what, not careful, not in the manner of Europeans, but concerned about waste since I was a child. People think I'm lying when I say that my earliest memory is of Jimmy Carter appearing on television during the OPEC crisis, but it's true. He sat, as I recall, in front of a fireplace in which burned a few small logs, and in a quiet drawl I still consider the very voice of reason-ableness, if not reason itself, he urged Americans to turn their thermostats down to sixty-eight degrees. Put on a sweater, he said, pulling on the placket of the gray cardigan that, along with two destroyed helicopters and seven dead bodies in the middle of the Iranian desert, would become a symbol of his political inepti-tude. The cardigan might have been light blue actually, the number of bodies in the desert higher or lower than seven, but the one detail I've never forgotten is the temperature, sixty-eight, if only because it happened to be the year of my birth. Sixty-eight degrees and a sweater—not sixty-seven and thermal underwear, not sixty-nine and a T-shirt. Perhaps the only thing that bothered me about my flat in London was that the thermostat was scored in Celsius, and several months into my stay, in my own sweater—and scarf sometimes, and open-fingered gloves—I still worried that I was wasting energy, that irretrievable kilowatts were push-ing through the warped glass and wind-rattled frame of my living room's big bay window and evaporating into the gray gray *gray* winter sky that hung above London like a shroud, but all I did was buy a set of heavy curtains to help retain the heat. By then I

was more worried about Derek, about, I should say, my relationship with him, which had taken on a pattern that seemed a little
too familiar for comfort: the phone call from work, the quick fuck
between five-thirty and six, the occasional drink at Benjy's or
some gay venue in Brixton or Islington or Shepherd's Bush—
places, as my guidebook told me, distinctly not on the beaten gay
track—and finally I just asked him if there was someone else. Not
exactly, he said. Not exactly? Well, he said, the truth is there is
someone. *You're* someone else. He didn't call for a week after
that, but he did call eventually, and he said he had an extra ticket
for a play on the South Bank, Friday, he said, eight sharp. Did I
want to go? In the end I was early; he was late. I'd wanted to ask
him how he came to possess an "extra" ticket for a play, but
immediately he said Derek's ill, meaning, I realized with a start,
the someone measured against whom I was someone else. He
grinned sardonically when he said it, and I wondered if he were
on to my ruse, if he'd found something with my real name on it
in my flat, or if he was merely playing a joke of his own, but
before I could question him we were rushed into the theater by
the usher, just as the curtain lifted. Coffee? Derek said afterward,
and I assented, picturing some dark firelit café where jazz would
be playing softly, more West Village than West London, really,
but it didn't matter, really, since what I got was one of the garishly
antiseptic eateries at the theater complex itself. One espresso
later—served in an unbelievably over-designed demitasse made
of bleached white paper complete with a glued-on handle whose
wings folded open and shut like a butterfly's—and Derek said, I
have to be off. I started to protest but he said, My patient calls,

and then he shook my hand with mock formality, winked, and told me to be a good boy and use the loo before I got on the tube. He nodded at a door behind me. Another espresso—the counter girl looked at me strangely when I presented my paper cup to be refilled, They're not free you know, she said, to which I replied, I *know*—and I headed for the door Derek had indicated. It led to a hallway that led to a long narrow descending staircase that led in turn to another hallway, this one dim, dirty, and smelling of subterranean damp, at the end of which was a door marked *Gentlemen*. There was no *Ladies* to be seen. I went through the loudly protesting door, and then, three feet farther on, another, just as loud, and found a small room containing three sinks and three stalls. No urinals. I almost turned around but by then I really did have to go, so I stepped into a stall. What a waste, I thought, addressing Derek in my head, 5.0 litres per flush as the Armitage Shanks commode dutifully indicated in faint periwinkle stencil, all for a thin piddle that would hardly fill one of those ridiculously wasteful paper demitasses used upstairs, and almost at the same time as I noticed the hole chiseled into the wall next to the toilet roll dispenser I heard the delayed double whine of the outer doors, and I knew why Derek had sent me down here. The stalls were partitioned by what looked like granite, a brown stone mottled with black and white and flecked here and there with purple, their doors were oak and heavy—solid, I mean, not mere veneer—and brightly varnished, and they reached all the way to the floor; the toilet was, in fact, rather more grand than the poured concrete structure twenty or thirty feet overhead, a structure that just happened to be the preeminent theatrical venue in the country, by which I mean that it wasn't exactly the place one would expect to find a glory hole, let alone one so laboriously, even lovingly constructed: perfectly round, its edges invitingly soft, and placed at an appropriately average height. The door to the stall next to mine opened, shut, its lock clicked. For a moment I heard only the hum of fluorescent lights, then, distinctly, the sound of a zipper opening, but nothing else, no plash of liquid into the bowl, no jingle of coins and car keys as pants slid down thighs, and so, after a moment, I bent over and risked a peek. All I saw at first was another hole in the wall opposite mine, and then, almost on cue, into the circular frame stepped a pair of dark trousers from whose open fly protruded an erect uncircumcised penis. A brown hand was stroking the penis, which was a slightly darker brown, and when it seemed to me that my own silence had grown conspicuously long my neighbor also bent forward, and our eyes met. I could see just one—it was dark and bright—and a large nose, and a full-lipped mouth that smiled almost immediately, revealing the inevitability of tea-stained teeth. He stood up, and a moment later his penis poked through the hole in the granite partition, but before I could decide what to do with it, or about it, the entrance doors whined in warning and the penis was gone like a mouse retreating into its hole. Faint footsteps, then silence. Then the water began running in the sink and I knew instinctively that we were fine: who washes their hands before they use the toilet? Well, the British probably do, but I wasn't thinking that then. The water ran; the penis reappeared; for some reason the sound was the license I needed, and without hesitating I took it, first in my hand and then in my mouth. The water continued to run. I closed my eyes against the kaleidoscopic spangles of the granite wall so close to my face. The thing in my mouth seemed to have no odor, no taste even: it simply felt. Warm. Living. Not even human really, just . . . alive. The granite was cold against my forehead when I let it rest there, and my urine in the bowl gave off a faint stink, making me wish I'd flushed. When the man twitched a bit, a warning or an invitation depending on your point of view, I moved aside; when he came his semen shot straight into the bowl and I couldn't quite suppress a chuckle; when, a moment later, I stepped out of the stall, unconsciously wiping my lips with the back of my hand, I saw a dainty little thing, tight pants, tight shirt, both black and shiny, crowned by a bleached-blond Caesar, standing at the sink where the water was still running down the drain at the rate of one gallon, one British gallon, per minute. I went right up to him and turned off the tap. That's very wasteful, I said, especially given the fact that we're in the middle of a drought. A moment later the man from the other stall joined us. He was Indian, about my age, more handsome than I would have expected from this sort of encounter, and taller than I'd realized; he must have had to bend his knees awkwardly to make it through the hole. As we walked out together the queen at the sink said, Greedy, greedy, greedy, in what I think was a Brummie accent, *Grey*-dy, *grey*-dy, *grey*-dy, and then he turned the water back on. My trick's name was Nigel. He carried a briefcase, wore a loosened tie; he was on his way home from an incredibly late day at the office, he said, and thought he'd check out the cottages on the South Bank before catching the tube at Embankment. My good luck, I said. It's usually busier, he said, but the play got bad notices. The play? I said, barely able to remember it. You're American? he said. I assumed he'd noticed my accent, but instead he squeezed my shoulder. Americans are just so big, he said, all that conspicuous consumption, and then, before we'd made it up the long flight of stairs, he'd told me about a few other places, Russell Square, the second floor toilets at Harvey Nicks, Mile End Park on Sunday nights, but the place that caught my ear was the Stoke Newington cemetery. People have sex in a cemetery? I said. What else are they going to do there? Nigel said, and then he made me hold back for a minute so we weren't seen leaving together. He kissed me first, said he was sorry he hadn't returned the favor but the boyfriend was waiting at home, and then he grabbed my crotch. Damn, he said. What a waste, and then, with an all-purpose Cheers mate, he was gone. Upstaged then, by not one but two boyfriends, I made my way home. Mile End, as it happened, was the next tube stop past mine, and I decided to ride the extra distance to take a look at the thin spit of trees at the north end of the park across from the station, a tiny copse that, according to Nigel, held as many as two dozen men each Sunday after Benjy's let out. I wasn't looking for another trick, but between Derek and Nigel I felt all worked up and there wasn't anything in particular to rush home to, and it was only a little before midnight when I spilled out of the tube with a large loud number of kids on their way to Benjy's—straight kids, because Benjy's only catered to a gay crowd on Sundays, and then only surreptitiously—and I let myself ride their swell for half a dozen steps until I saw the trees across the street, low scrubby evergreens fleshing out the trunks of some kind of short deciduous with pale shiny bark. Stick-skinny girls in short skirts shivered in the cold October wind while boys with acne on their foreheads tossed their keys up in the air and looked around to see if anyone was watching, and measured against their camaraderie the little grove looked cold and inhospitable, but still, I decided to check it out. The nearest entrance to the park was a ways in on Burdett Road, past Benjy's and a busy chip shop and the back of a darkened dingy council block, and after I'd made it through all that—I was sure that everyone I passed knew exactly what I was up to, and walking through them felt like running a gauntlet—I had to walk back up to the trees across a lawn whose grass was so dry it broke audibly under my feet. The papers said it had been, literally, the driest summer in recorded history, and though fall had brought the relief of coolness the gray skies hadn't yet delivered any rain. The drought had been some kind of vague comfort to me during my several months here. At first I thought it was simply because it reinforced my natural urge to conserve resources and ration them appropriately. Each evening as I washed my handful of dishes with a barely dampened sponge I watched the news on Channel 4 and felt joined with like-minded liberals all over England. The lawns of Hyde Park browned like toast, black cabs withered beneath a never-washed patina of dust, and swimming pools—said to be in Oxfordshire, although I had a hard time imagining something as American as a swimming pool anywhere in England—filled at summer's start, were by now nothing more than puddles at the bottom of dirt-encrusted concrete holes, and, as I said, I felt a kinship with these people, which had comforted me, or at least I thought it had. I would watch the news and give the taps an extra twist to make sure they were fully closed and imagine my downstairs neighbor doing exactly the same thing, but as I walked across the open lawn of Mile End Park I remembered that New York, like London now, had been in the midst of a drought when I'd moved there a decade earlier, and I realized that it was probably only memory that assuaged my loneliness, not recycled water but recycled thoughts, recycled habits: letting laundry accumulate, showering every other day, putting a brick in the toilet tank to save a quart of water—an American quart—with each flush. The moon was the single light in the night sky bright enough to push through the clouds, and I felt its beam focused on me as I crunched my way across the wide open lawn. When I was on the street the trees had seemed slightly sinister but now they cast friendly sheltering shadows, and as I got closer I could make out several gaps in the low evergreens. I headed for the nearest, pushed aside a few scaly branches, and suddenly found myself on a well-worn path. A mulch of last year's needles and leaves softened my footsteps, which only three or four paces further on brought me to a small oblong clearing, where, like socks on a laundry line, a row of more than a dozen condoms hung over a couple of thin branches. Or flags, I thought. The condoms hung there like a row of welcoming banners in front of a swanky hotel, although that night the clearing was without any guests. It was surprisingly bright though. The branches overhead did little more than filter the moon's glow, and plastic wrappers from condoms and candy glittered like something more precious than mere trash while patiently waiting out their millennia on earth. A flash on a

tree trunk caught my eye: a shred of red cloth. I tried to imagine
the man who had leaned up against this trunk and what had
caused him to tear his shirt, perhaps a startled twitch as a pair of
headlights shone through the leaves, or the inevitable shudder as
he came, or perhaps the grove had simply held on to a piece of
him when he walked away, unwilling to take the tryst as lightly as
he had, as had the men who'd draped the condoms across its
branches. A pair of voices disturbed me then. Peering through
the trees, I could make out a couple of stout men passing by on
the sidewalk, which couldn't have been twenty feet away. Their
blond crewcuts reflected the moon like mirror balls—almost all
the white men in this neighborhood were blond and crewcut, just
as almost all their South Asian neighbors wore their hair long,
either beneath turbans or, on the younger men, in neatly dressed
ponytails—and their East London accent was so pronounced I
could hardly make out a word, but the tone was loud and boister-
ous, drunken but not particularly so. I imagined they were
making their way home from the pub to their wives, and as their
voices faded away they were replaced by the memory of another
disembodied voice, this one also loud, but angry, shouting actually, I was only taking a *piss*, is what the voice had shouted. Can't
someone take a piss without you shutting the light off behind
them? and I remembered shouting back, I piss in the dark all the
time, even though the light I had shut off had been in the living
room. Some people, I shouted, don't need to look at their dicks
to make them work, and a moment later the voice and the body
from which it emanated appeared in the door. Well, some of us
should clean up the mess we make beside the toilet in the middle

of the night, is what he said. I'm just trying to do my part, I said then, to which he replied, This isn't a play. There are no parts, there isn't a script. There are only lights, which we leave on so we can see where we're *going*—and just then a car's headlights splintered the grove of trees, dancing a chorus line of skeletal shadows across the clearing where I stood. I shook myself and pretended I was shivering. As a memory, it was simply a piece of trash, and, dutifully, I shoved it back in the bin and slammed the lid down on it. I pocketed the scrap of red cloth and headed for home, and when I got there I showered off the coating of dust I seemed to have acquired on my foray into the woods. I felt guilty that I couldn't bring myself to shower as someone told me they did in Germany—a quick spray, a lather with soap that congealed perceptibly as the water evaporated from one's body, a second splash to rinse. I'd tried it only once, on what seemed like a hot summer morning, and when I stepped out of the shower my teeth were chattering and my skin slimy with soap scum, and as I toweled off I looked longingly at the spume of steam that, along with a falsetto caterwaul, rose from my downstairs neighbor's bathroom window. That night I indulged myself, lingering in the shower for nearly ten minutes, but afterwards I turned the heat all the way down and wrapped myself in a comforter I'd bought when I'd bought my bed, and I said, out loud, defiantly, I *am* doing my part. In the morning I saw that Derek had called the night before, while I'd been in the park, and he came by later that afternoon to make it up to me. It's fucking freezing, he said when he arrived, and with a carelessness that I envied he rotated the dial on the thermostat without even looking at it. By the time he left the sun had gone down and my flat was so hot my eyes watered in their sockets. I turned the thermostat down, blindly, as Derek had turned it up, but it wasn't until I woke up shivering that I realized my place was, once again, freezing, and empty, and life went on that way, it got even colder but still neither rain nor snow would fall, I saw Derek once a week on average, a quick meal usually, followed by a quick fuck, although sometimes he sneaked out on a weekend and we would go shopping, Oxford Street, Covent Garden and Soho, South Ken, and I blew hundreds of pounds on those occasions but it didn't really matter because in between days with Derek I was writing the most puerile sorts of advertising copy masking itself as cinematic entertainment, for which money was simply being thrown at me, and even at an unfavorable exchange rate I had cash to burn. And so it happened that I woke up one morning after Derek had been there the night before and saw that, Derek or no Derek, my flat was hardly empty. I looked around my bedroom, through the doors to the front room. There were things everywhere. Electronics equipment especially: television, VCR, stereo, computer, printer, fax, phone, the answering machine with its unblinking red eye. Stacks of books grew from the mantel up the chimney, flanked by a pair of candleless candlesticks I'd picked up in the market on Brick Lane, and in the grate itself was a chest I'd bought the same day to hold the British linens I'd bought to cover my British mattress, which, like British paper and British men, was longer and skinnier than the American variety. I remembered then the list of my possessions I'd made in my first week here, and draped by my comforter I made my way to my desk and sat in my chair and turned on my computer—so many things!—and tried to recreate it. I stopped after thirty pages. I hadn't looked in the closet yet, or pulled open a single drawer, but I didn't need to: it was clear I had somehow managed to stuff my flat as fat as a Thanksgiving turkey, and I remembered then what Nigel had said about Americans and their conspicuous consumption. For the first time I wondered what would happen to all of my possessions when I left. I tripped on that for a moment, I wasn't sure why, until I realized it was the first time I'd acknowledged that just as surely as I'd come to London I'd leave it one day, I wasn't sure when and I wasn't sure why, but then I wasn't exactly sure why I'd come to London either. I'd thought I wanted to live unburdened by the things that had weighed me down in New York, but as I scrolled through the list on my computer—I couldn't bring myself to waste the paper it would take to print it out—it seemed to me that life was nothing more than a process of accumulation. The only thing you lost was time. But I refused to accept this conclusion, and I resolved, again, to divest myself of as much extraneous matter as possible, months of newspapers that had accumulated and needed to be recycled, the books I'd read, which I sold to a used bookstore for a few pounds, also a nested stack of electronics boxes that took up almost all the space in my closet. Why did I save this stuff, I asked myself as I snapped the boxes' Styrofoam packing sleeves into tiny pieces, why did I think a minor act of conservation could repair the damage already perpetrated by the manufacturing process that had belched forth all this shit? Also in my closet were a couple of shirts that had come from New York with me, shirts I'd rarely worn there and never worn here, and I decided I would give them to the Salvation Army. The nearest one I could find was in Camden, which required a formidably complex tube journey, but I negotiated it successfully, and handed over the two shirts plus a couple more that I'd bought for Derek and that he'd said he couldn't accept, and a pair of pants he'd bought me that I liked but still shucked out of spite, and as I handed my package over I told myself that I was becoming one of those faceless people who provide all the great finds in used clothing stores that I'd been adept at sniffing out in my first years in New York. It was an image of myself I liked, and so the circuitous route between Bethnal Green and Camden became a regular sojourn for me. I only went when I had bought something, a jacket or a pair of pants or shoes, and all I did was weed out a similar older item to make room for the new thing, and I hadn't realized how frequent a visitor I was until one day when I went in armed with a single pair of green cotton chinos, and, because I felt silly going in to surrender one item, a white button-down shirt that I would have had to replace sooner or later, and the old woman whom I saw most regularly smiled at me and said, Simon will be glad you've been in. Simon? I said, and the old woman beamed. He works at the weekend. He's just your size—he usually snatches up whatever you bring in before it makes it to the floor. Says you keep him in clothes, you do. Even shoes. I mumbled something incoherently then, I wasn't even sure what I'd meant my mumbling to sound like, and quickly left the store, but that weekend, after an early meeting with Derek, I found myself in front of the Salvation Army. There was the thinnest coat of frost on the ground—the weatherman tried to call it snow, but no one was fooled—and I'd worn sunglasses to protect my eyes from the glare. I kept them on when I went into the store, thinking they would serve as some sort of disguise, but when I realized that Simon would have no idea who I was I took them off quickly. There was no mistaking him though. The green and brown plaid shirt he wore had come from my closet, as well as the brown corduroy pants, and although I couldn't see Simon's feet I guessed he was wearing a pair of suede boots I'd dropped off on the same day I dropped off the plaid shirt and corduroys. Excuse me, I said then. I was in here earlier this week and I saw a pair of pants I liked. They were green. Canvas, no pleats. Simon looked up from the book he'd been reading. Sorry? Despite myself, I was surprised. He was young—I mean, much younger than I was—and a part of me had expected my own face to look at me from out of my own clothes. Green pants, I said quickly, stammering slightly. I saw them earlier—I don't work during the week, Simon interrupted me. Wouldn't know what was here, but I don't remember no green *pants* in, what was it, *can*vas? He stressed the words slightly, and I wasn't sure if he was mocking the words themselves, or just the way I'd said them, but then he laughed lightly, waved an arm, said, We've got loads of polyester to choose from, and as he spoke he turned his book over and placed it open-faced on the counter, a college textbook, economics. He didn't even look like a younger version of me. His hair was floppy and brown and darkened by a tinge of grease, whereas my hair was crewed like the men in my neighborhood. Derek had teased me when I first cut it off, asked me if I was trying to score with the skinheads down at the local, but then he'd grown serious and run his hand over my downy head and said, It suits you. It suits you, I guess, though I think you deserve the luxury of hair, but still, I continued to buzz it: I'd bought the clippers after all, and couldn't let them go to waste. I shook my head then, to clear it. I'm sure I saw them, I insisted. I even remember the size: thirty-two in the waist and inseam both. Simon's expression was puzzled and uncomfortable. He shrugged thin shoulders inside the green and brown plaid shirt. Maybe they sold. The collar of the shirt had darkened from the grease in his hair, and he pulled at it now, nervously, and I felt sweat filming my own neck beneath my scarf. I placed my hands flat on the counter. Could you check in the back? Maybe they were taken off the rack for some reason. Look, Simon said, we don't take stuff off the floor unless we're holding it for— That's it! I said. I asked her to hold it for me. What's her name, the old woman. Trudy, Simon said. His voice was suddenly suspicious. That's right, Trudy. I could feel the sweat coursing down my neck now, wetting my shirt inside my winter coat. I could feel the redness of my face and the pounding of my heart. Trudy put it back for me, along with a white shirt. A button-down. Simon stared at me now, disbelief written plainly on his face. Trudy's holding a pair of green trousers for you, and a white shirt? I just nodded my head then. I couldn't bring myself to speak, nor even to meet his gaze. My eyes caught the cracked spine of his textbook, saw a yellow sticker, itself creased into near illegibility: USED. Just a minute, I heard Simon say, and as he walked from the counter I watched for his feet. There were the boots. I felt a thrill up and down my spine when I saw them, and a knot in my stomach as well, and then Simon was back with the same brown bag in which I'd delivered the clothes. It was stapled closed now, and the word *Simon* was written on it in black magic marker, and the man who bore that name, and my clothes as well, dropped the bag on the counter. Here you go. I still couldn't look at him. I grabbed the bag and turned for the door, but Simon's voice stopped me. All right, hold on. I turned slowly. Yes? Simon's face and voice were flat when he spoke, but his knuckles were white where his hands gripped the counter's edge. That'll be a fiver, he said. I'm sorry? I said. That's five for the trousers, Simon said again. He paused. And five for the shirt. I thought of protesting, but didn't. What could I say: But they're mine? I thought of running out of the store then, even jerked a little towards the door, and Simon jerked when I jerked, not as if to follow, not even in imitation: it was as if his body was attached to mine by the threads woven into the clothes he wore. Slowly, I returned to the counter. I pulled two fives from my wallet and fingered them for a moment. They were fresh from a cash machine, crisp, sharp-edged. You could cut your finger on these, I thought. I thought, This is how much it costs. It wasn't very much, even if I was buying something that already belonged to me. I gave the boy called Simon the money. Brazen now, Simon put the money in the pocket of the corduroy pants. I looked at him a moment longer. They all fit you. Even the shoes. Something changed in Simon's face then. Disgust gave way momentarily to shame, and then, quickly, anger rose up again. Aw, go on, get out of here before I call a copper. His voice—young, high-pitched, almost cracking under the strain—wasn't convincing, but I nodded curtly and left. Outside it was cold and bright and I squinted against the glare until I remembered my sunglasses and covered my eyes. The bag with Simon's name on it dangled loosely in one hand, and as I walked toward the tube station I remembered something else Derek had said not so long ago, when I'd tried to tell him that my name wasn't actually Derek. I'd stuttered my way around the subject until, eventually, I realized that he'd figured it out long ago, and that he hadn't cared. What he'd said was that some things, like names, can be used over and over again—or bodies for that matter. But then he went on. He said, Some things *can't* be used twice. There are some things, he said, that are used up on the first go-round, and whatever's left behind, if anything, is just pollution. There's no point in saving it, he said, or reusing it, it's just left over, and as he spoke his hands were on my shoulders and he was looking me straight in the eye, and I felt as though he were telling me *I* was one of those things that can be used only once. People like Derek, I thought, people like Nigel, they were able to have boyfriends and still find the time for trysts on the side, and tricks, whereas it was all I could manage to be someone's someone else. They renewed themselves endlessly, shed the days like skin cells and grew new ones without even thinking about it, while all I could do was fade away slowly as though I were simply semi-biodegradable packaging whose contents had long since been consumed, and suddenly I felt the bag with someone else's name on it hanging from my arm like a dead weight. Why did you keep coming back then? is what I'd said to Derek—it was what I had said in New York—and Derek had said, I never left, and the more I thought of his words the less I could make of them. In New York it had been worse. In New York it had been: I was never really here, and what can you say to that? I stopped walking then; I'd gone far past the tube station; I looked around and saw, in fact, that I had no idea where I was. But even the strangeness was familiar from my first days here, it brought with it a familiar elation and a familiar dejection, but I threw all these old feelings away, and threw away my old clothes as well, dropped them in the first bin I came across, and then I turned toward what I thought was the east and set out on foot for my flat. I got lost, of course. Of course I got lost: for London is laid out as haphazardly as a warren. It's a myriad of Streets High and Low, of Courts and Cloisters and Crescents and full Circles, Paths and Parks and Parkways, and Yards, and Mews, and Quays, Palaces and Castles and Mansions and Halls and mere Houses (never so mere in reality), and Drives (which sounds creepingly American to my ears, and suburban at that), there are Ways to go and Ends to be arrived at, Barrows and Buries—or would it be Burys?—Moats to be crossed and Bridges to cross them, also Brydges, which don't seem to cross anything, and Squares, which rarely are, and all of this (and much, much more) is further complicated by a strange feud between lexicography and cartography, so that what is here a Road becomes, a few feet farther on, a Terrace; a Vale might become a Walk or broaden suddenly into a Mall, Groves are treeless, Gardens without plants, Gates nowhere to be found. London is, in other words, a maze, but I was simply amazed, surprised that it had taken me so long to realize I was lost. But it was why I'd come here after all, to lose myself in a foreign place. That seems, now, just another way of saying that I wanted to throw myself away, and if I didn't actually succeed it's probably only because it's against my nature to litter.

—1999

V.

There are moments of great lucidity and moments even I recognize as delusional, but most of the time I linger somewhere between. Is this death opening the door for me, I wonder sometimes, or life, holding on to me? Holding me back. I feel as if I've been made privy to a new aspect of human existence and I'm tortured by its beauty, and by the fact that it's probably not real. The pressure to believe weighs so heavily at the end. To believe in this bed, this room, this city. To believe in the people walking outside my window and their migratory thoughts, sitting on my sill like a bird at a feeder, offering a glimpse of themselves but taking away one more kernel of my life. I am being pecked to death. I am being eaten. But in return I am becoming a man of visions. My body is too insubstantial to hold back the thoughts and feelings of my fleshier fellow citizens, and they flood into me. But will my death dissolve them, or finally allow them to become real?

Dues

First of all, Adam. He creaked up beside me on a bicycle that looked like it had been welded out of leftover plumbing parts. Pull over, he said with all the authority of a keystone cop.

He was cute enough. In particular, the hair: black, thick, sticking out of his head in a dozen directions. Long thin legs straddled the flared central strut of his bicycle like denim-covered tent poles and he stared down at my own bike with eyes the color of asphalt—the old gray kind, with glass embedded in it to reflect light.

But this wasn't a pick-up.

That is my bicycle, he announced. A trace of an accent?

I don't think so, I said. I paid for this bike.

Then you paid for stolen merchandise, he said, his consonants soft, Eastern European. *Shtolen mershendise.* I think you should show me where.

I'D GONE ON a tip. Benny's East Village. You won't believe his prices, a friend told me. Isn't that the burrito place? I said. In fact my friend had said, They're probably all stolen, but what you don't know won't hurt you. He steals burritos? *Bicycles*, my friend said. Come *on*.

By the time Adam and I arrived the shop had closed for the day. Adam's thin legs labored to turn his creaking pedals, and it occurred to me I could have outrun him, but I didn't. The sun was setting at our backs and our shadows stretched out in front of us like twinned towers. I thought we were a pair. I thought we were in it together.

Benny sat on a swivel chair on the sidewalk, a television propped in front of him on a pair of milk crates; a tin of rice and beans wobbled on his lap. We'd been there only a few minutes when a man half carried, half pushed a bike up the street. He held it by the seat, lifting the back wheel off the ground because it couldn't turn: it was locked to the frame. After inspecting the bicycle, Benny paid the man from a roll of bills he pulled from the breast pocket of his T-shirt, stowed the bicycle under the grate of his store, and returned to his chair.

I turned to Adam.

I guess I should have investigated further.

You should have.

He was pulling his kryptonite U-lock from his belt, and I inferred from this action that he wanted to trade bikes. I dismounted, and was unwinding my chain from the seat post when his lock caught me in the side of the head. Fireflies streaked through my field of vision when the lock struck me, but I didn't actually lose consciousness until the sidewalk hit me in the forehead.

CHARLIE SPONGED THE grit from my face. What was stuck to solid skin washed away easily, but the bits of gravel embedded in the gashes on my cheek and forehead had to be convinced to relinquish their berth. I closed my eyes against the water trickling from his rag.

One summer when I was seven or eight I carried cupfuls of water from a stream and poured them down chipmunk holes. The chipmunks would remain underground for as long as possible until, wobbling like drunken sailors, they staggered into the sunshine. I would lift them gently into a tinfoil turkey tray I'd habitated with rocks, plants, a ribbed tin can laid on its side (a sleeping den, I'd thought), and then I'd watch as the chipmunks revived, explored their playground tentatively, and then, inevitably, hurdled the shiny wall and scrambled back down their holes.

I'm afraid I'm going to have to use a tweezers for the last of it.

I opened my eyes. Charlie was making a face, as if performing this surgery hurt him instead of me.

He asked if he was hurting me.

I was still remembering the way the last chipmunk had lain on its side after I'd fished it from its home, eyes closed, chest fluttering as rapidly as a bee's wings. I'd dared to stroke its heaving ribs. The chipmunk curled itself into a ball around my finger, its mouth and the claws of all four paws digging at me until I flung it away and it scurried to safety.

It hurts, I said, then caught Charlie's arm as he flinched. My head hurts, I said. What you're doing doesn't hurt.

BENNY'S SOLD BIKES every day except Sunday from eleven until seven, but was always to be bustling with activity. In the mornings a young woman worked on the bicycles. This was Deneisha, who seemed to live on the third floor. Every ten minutes a younger version of her leaned out the window to relay a request: Deneisha, Mami says why you didn't get no more coffee if you used the last of it? Deneisha, Benny says to call him back on his cell phone *now*. Deneisha, Eduardo wants to know when are you gonna take the training wheels off my bike so I can go riding with him? Deneisha, her thick body covered in greasy overalls, inky black spirals of hair rubberbanded off her smooth round face, ignored these interruptions, working with Allen wrenches and oil cans and tubes of glue on gears, brakes, tires. For bicycles that still had a chain fastened to them she had an enormous pair of snips, their handles as long as her meaty arms, and for U-locks she had a saw that threw sparks like a torch as it chewed through tempered steel.

After the shop closed there was a lull until the sun went down, and then the bicycles began to arrive. Every thief was different. Some skulked, others paraded their booty openly, offering it to anyone they passed on the sidewalk, but few spent any time bargaining with Benny. The more nervous the thief, the less interest Benny showed, the less money he pulled from the roll of bills. He seemed completely untroubled by his illicit enterprise, absorbing stolen bikes with the same equanimity with which he consumed tins and cartons of delivered food. Only the white kids, the college-aged junkies selling off the first or the last of their ties to a suburban past, tried his patience. I said ten bucks, I heard him say once. Take it or leave it.

CHARLIE COULDN'T UNDERSTAND my obsession. We'd only been together three months, and what I'd learned about him was that he took in information with a stenographer's zen. Existence is the sum of experience, he'd shrugged that first night, as if the events of our lives were drops of water and we the puddles at the end of their runneled paths, little pools of history. When I still wouldn't let it go he prodded harder.

Is it the coincidence that bothers you, or the fact that he hit you? Or is it that you pretended innocence of what you were getting when you bought the bike in the first place, and now it's come back and bitten you in the ass? Or—he kissed my bandage gently—whupped you upside the head?

At the time I couldn't answer him, and hindsight makes it that much less clear. I offered him words like *cleave* and *hew*, words that could mean both cutting and binding, but Charlie waved my rhetoric away. Context makes meaning clear, he said. Then, more bluntly: *Choose.*

But I couldn't choose. My life felt splayed on either side of the incident with Adam like his long thin legs straddling the ancient bicycle—which he did, in fact, leave for me. Like conjoined twins, my two selves were linked at the hip, sharing a common future but divided as to which past to claim. And so every day I rode Adam's creaking iron bike to a stoop across from Benny's and waited for something like Deneisha's saw to sever my old unmolested self, leaving my new scarred body to get on with things.

AT A PARTY Charlie dragged me to I told the story behind the bandages on my cheek and forehead a half dozen times. By then the two bruises had joined into one, across my brow, down the left side of my face, vanishing into the hairline. The single bruise was mottled black, purple, blue, green, yellow, but, like the story I told over and over again, had become essentially painless, and as the night wore on Charlie added his own coda to my words. Victim, he would say, turning my mottled left profile to the audience. Thief, he said, showing them my right.

Uh oh, he said at one point, here comes trouble. *Trouble* was a man around our age, one hand holding shaggy bangs off his unlined forehead as though he were taking in a sight, the Grand Canyon, a caged animal. From across the room I heard his cry. Now *where* did I leave that man? His gaze fell on Charlie. *There he is.*

Charlie introduced him as Fletcher: his ex-boyfriend, who'd dumped Charlie last summer after a five-year relationship that Charlie referred to by the names of various failed political unions: Czechoslovakia, Upper and Lower Egypt, the Austro-Hungarian Empire. His arms around Charlie's waist, Fletcher pulled him a few feet away, as if together they were examining my bruised face. Is this *really* the new model, Fletcher said, or just something you picked up at Rent-a-Wreck? Charlie offered me a wan smile but, like the Orangeman that he was, seemed content in Fletcher's possessive embrace. Under his questions, I recited once again the story of the two bicycles, the single blow, adding this time the week of camping out across from Benny's shop. Fletcher's assessment: I don't know why you're focusing on the Puerto Rican, he's just a businessman. It was the Slav who sucker-punched you.

ON THE BICYCLE ride to Benny's, Adam told me he came from Slovenia. He came here on a student visa, stayed on after his country seceded from the Yugoslavian republic; that was a decade ago. Back home, he told me, the terrain is hills and mountains but everyone rides bicycles like this. He smacked the flecked chrome of his handlebars. Often you see people, not just grandmothers but healthy young men, pushing their bicycles up inclines too steep to pedal. I wanted a mountain bike.

He told me he was illegal, worked without a green card, had almost to live like a thief himself; he had a degree in computer science and an MBA, had emigrated to get in on the dot-com boom but ended up tending bar at Windows on the World. After Fletcher's harangue I bought two books on Balkan history at the Strand, a novel and a book of journalism, and I read them on the stoop across from Benny's in an effort to understand what Adam meant by telling me about his stunted furtive existence, the two kinds of bicycles, the broadside with the lock. Why *did* he need a mountain bike, if he was only going to ride the swamp-flat streets of the East Village?

BUT THEN: GRACE.

I was sitting on the stoop across from Benny's absorbed in the cyclical tale of centuries of avenged violence that is Balkan history. Two plaster lions flanked me, their fangs dulled beneath years of brown paint. A woman stopped in front of me and hooked a finger around one of the lion's incisors. That is a *great* book, she said with the kind of enthusiasm only a middle-aged counterculturalist can summon. She pointed not to the book I was reading but to the novel on the concrete beside me. Against the heat of early September she wore green plastic sandals, black spandex shorts, a halter top sewn from a threadbare bandanna.

The spandex was worn and semitransparent on her thin thighs and her stomach was so flat it was concave; a ruby glowed from her navel ring, an echo of the bindi on her forehead. She could have been thirty or fifty. She let go of the lion's tooth and picked up the novel even as I told her I looked forward to reading it. Like, wow, she exclaimed, and when she blinked it seemed to me her eyes were slightly out of sync. She held the book up to me, the cover propped open to the first set of endpapers. An ex libris card was stuck on the left-hand side with a name penned on it in black ink: *Grace* was the first name, followed by a polysyllabic scrawl ending in *-itz*. The same card adorned the book I was reading and, nervously, my index finger traced the hard shell of scab above my left eye. What she said next would have seemed no more unlikely had the lion behind her spoken it himself: That's *my* name.

SHE DIDN'T ASK for her books back—they weren't stolen, she'd bought them for a class at the New School and sold them afterwards so she could afford a course in elementary Sanskrit— but I insisted she take them anyway, sensing that a drama was unfolding somewhat closer than the Balkans. In the end she accepted the novel but told me to finish the history. Over coffee I told her about Adam and the bicycle, and Grace was like, wow.

Once I got the same cabdriver twice, she said. She blinked: her left eye and then, a moment later, her right. I mean, I got in a cab with a driver I'd had before. I tried to ask him if he'd ever, you know, randomly picked up the same person twice, besides me of course, but he didn't speak English so I don't know. Her face clouded for a moment, then lit up again. Blink blink. Oh and then once I got in the same car on the F train. I went to this winter solstice party out in Park Slope, and the kicker is we went to a bar afterward so I didn't even leave from the same stop I came out on. I think I got off at Fourth Avenue or whatever it is, and then we walked all the way to like Seventh or something, it was fucking freezing is all I remember, but whatever. When the train pulled into the station it was the same train I'd ridden out on, the same car. Totally spooky, huh?

How'd you know it was the same one?

Graffiti, duh. *Hector loves Isabel.* Scratched into the glass with a razor blade in, like, really big letters.

And the cabdriver?

His name was Jesus.

Just Jesus?

Just Jesus.

THE INCIDENT WITH Adam had been painful but finite. A city tale, one of those chance meetings leading to romance or, in this case, violence; already the bruise was fading. But the incident with Grace was more troubling, awoke in me a creeping dread. What if life was just a series of borrowed items, redundant actions, at best repetitious, at worst theft? "Those who cannot remember the past are condemned to repeat it." Okay, but what if repetition happened regardless of memory? What if we were all condemned? I felt then that I understood the history I was reading, began to sympathize with the urge to destroy something that continually reminded you of your derivative status. Like most people, I first bought used items out of poverty, but after my fortunes improved I continued to buy secondhand from a sense of a different debt. Clothes, books, bicycles: I wanted to pay my dues to history, wanted to wear it on my back, carry it in my hands, ride it through the streets. But now it seemed history had rejected my tithing, rejected it scornfully. The past can be sold, it mocked me, but it can never be bought.

CHARLIE WAS LESS blasé about Grace than he'd been about Adam, but ultimately dismissed it.

It takes three events to form a narrative. Two is just a coincidence.

But a coincidence that's made up of two coincidences. What's that?

Proof that New York, as someone once said, is just a series of small towns.

The first night, after cleaning and bandaging my wounds, Charlie put me to bed and spooned himself behind me, his arms around me, the outline of his erect penis palpable through two pairs of underwear. At the time it was so familiar I didn't really notice it, but later it came to preoccupy my thoughts. It was like Adam's mountain bike, misplaced, a tool for which the pertinent scenario existed only at a remembered remove. Or Grace's ex libris cards, a claim of ownership on something she had no intention of keeping, like a gravestone on a ghost's abandoned grave. The night I met Grace, Charlie and I had sex for the first time since Adam had whacked me in the head, and the whole time I was unable to shake an image of Fletcher's face next to Charlie's crotch. See this? This is *mine*. Later that night, when I was dozing off and Charlie was leafing through the book that had fallen from my hands, I suddenly sat up.

Fletcher.

What about Fletcher?

You used to belong to him. Silently but victoriously, I ticked off forefinger, middle finger, ring finger. Then: That's three.

THE NEXT DAY, after Charlie went to work, I stayed in the apartment. I worked in the morning, ordered lunch from an Italian place around the corner. I read while I ate tepid fettuccine and kept reading after I'd finished my meal. All this was normal, or had been normal, if you disregarded the weeks I'd spent in front of Benny's. On a pad made up of reused sheets from early drafts of stories was written "shaving cream, milk," but after I'd finished the history I neglected my shopping and instead took a nap. I didn't wake until Charlie called that evening after he got off work.

Dinner? There's that new French place on 12th.

Oh, I said. I'm sorry, I was hungry, I ordered in. Mexican.

That's fine, Charlie said. I've got some chicken in the fridge, and some work I really should get done. My place tonight?

Oh, I said again. I'm sorry. I, um. My head's pounding. Do you mind?

Charlie didn't say *that's fine* the second time. He said, Sure, and it seemed to me his voice wasn't annoyed but instead relieved. I'll give you a call tomorrow.

THE NEXT DAY I stayed in again, working. I'd been trying to write about Adam since I'd met him, but after I met Grace the story suddenly fell into place.

In the story I'm afraid to leave my apartment. I'm afraid that a stranger will stop me on the sidewalk and put his hand on my Salvation Army chest. That's my shirt. Someone else claims my pants. Nearly naked, I skulk indoors. But not even my home is safe. A visitor runs his hand over my sofa (Housing Works, $250). I used to *love* this couch. Another pulls open the drawers of my desk (Regeneration, $400): What *are* the odds? Finally someone waves their arms, taking in the time-smudged dimensions of my tiny apartment. This used to be *my* home. My throat is dry, I go to the faucet for a drink. But as the water runs I wonder: how many bodies has this passed through to get to me?

But it was worse than all that. When Charlie came over that evening he glanced through the story I'd written and said, Haven't I read this before?

ON THE THIRD day I didn't leave my apartment, Charlie called me and told me a story:

Once I wanted to hack all my hair off with a pair of scissors. But I had a crewcut at the time. So I went out and bought next year's calendar and marked the date a year hence with a big red X. For the next twelve months I didn't touch my hair, and when the day with the X came up I looked in the mirror and realized I liked my hair long. I realized that my crewcuts had been a way of hacking off my hair all along.

I said the only thing I could think of.

Huh?

Your whole shut-in thing, Charlie said. It's not real. Or it's not new. It's just a symbol of something you already do. You've already done. Think about it. Where is it you're *really* afraid to go?

I thought about it.

You have a crewcut now, I said.

Give me a break, will you? I'm going bald, it's the dignified thing to do.

WHEN WE MET Charlie gave me a road map. This was on our third date. Oh, okay, our second. We'd gone back to his apartment and he spread the map out on his kitchen table (IKEA, ninety-nine bucks). The table, like everything else in Charlie's apartment, was new and neat but the map was old and wrinkled, a flag-sized copy of the continental US, post-Alaska, pre-Hawaii. Some of the creases were so worn they'd torn, or were about to.

Now, Charlie said. Fold it.

There were four long creases, twelve short, and folding the map proved as hard as solving Rubik's cube. I got it wrong a half dozen times before I finally got the front and back covers in the right place and, a little chagrined, handed it to Charlie.

Did I fail?

You passed. With flying colors. Anyone who can fold a map on the first try is way too rational for me.

And what about people who can't fold one at all?

In answer, Charlie pulled open the white laminate-fronted drawer of one of those nameless pieces of furniture, a storage unit. Inside were several maps practically wadded up, as well as dozens of takeout menus and hundreds of crooked twist ties. He had to scrunch the pile down before the drawer would close again.

Wow, I said. The map test *and* your messy drawer. You must really like me.

Charlie grinned, sheepish but pleased. It's about time I entered into a new alliance.

By the time I understood what that meant, I thought I was ready to sign. And then Adam came along.

ON THE FOURTH day, Grace called. When I asked her how she'd gotten my number she said, Out of the book, and when I started to ask how she knew my last name she interrupted me and said, Honey, I think you'd better turn on the television.

MONTHS LATER, WHEN the indemnity claims began to be discussed in the press, New Yorkers would learn that the opposing sides, the insurance companies and the property owners, differed on a crucial issue: whether the collapse of the towers constituted one event, or two. The World Trade Center, it turned out, was insured for three billion dollars, but if it was deemed that the crash of the second plane into the south tower, not quite twenty minutes after the north tower was hit, constituted a distinct historical event, the insurers would have to pay the full amount twice, in effect saying that the buildings had been destroyed not once but two times. A lot of the argument, as it turned out, was rhetorical: to the insurers, the World Trade Center was a single site—maps marked it with a single X, guidebooks gave it only one entry—that had been destroyed by a united terrorist attack. But to the property owners, the Twin Towers were, architecturally, structurally, visibly, two buildings destroyed by two separate planes, either one of which could have missed its target. Which argument began to make more and more sense to me as time went on and details about what had happened came out. Nearly three quarters of the people who died were in the north tower, and, of those, more than ninety percent were on floors above those hit by the plane, including dozens of people attending a breakfast conference at Windows on the World. The reason why far fewer people died in the second tower, which stood for less than an hour, as opposed to the hundred minutes the north tower remained intact, is that people in the south tower saw what had happened to the north tower and evacuated their offices. Regardless of whether you considered the two plane crashes coincidence or concerted assault, the planes had struck separately—and people in the second incident had learned from the first.

THE ANTONYM TO history is prophecy. Historical patterns only emerge when we look back in time; they exist in the future as nothing more than guesses. That we make such projections speaks of a kind of faith, though whether that faith is in the past or the future, the predictability of human nature, or physics, or god, is anybody's guess. But in the end, it always takes you by surprise. By which I mean that when I fought my way through the clouds of dust and crowds of dusty people to Charlie's apartment, I found Fletcher had beaten me there. Who could have foreseen that?

IN THE DAYS to come, I rode my bike around the city, watched as walls and windows and trees and lampposts filled up with pictures of the missing. Dust clogged my lungs and coated the chain of Adam's creaking bicycle, making it harder and harder to turn the pedals, but it was three days before I stopped wandering aimlessly and actually started looking for him.

I found him, finally, a day and a half later, at the armory on Lexington and 26th. Indian restaurants lined that stretch of Lex, and the air was usually tinged with curry, but all the restaurants had been closed for days. There were thousands of pictures taped to the wall of the armory, hundreds of people queuing to look at them. Many of the pictures had smeared into unrecognizable blurs after two days of thunderstorms. Where there was a television crew, dozens of people holding up Polaroids and snapshots and flyers jockeyed to get on camera.

By common will the line moved from left to right. Heads nodded up and down as feet shuffled side to side. I tried not to look in anyone's eyes, living or photographed. I did look at the living, just in case, but mostly I looked at the pictures on the wall.

Sometimes A leads to Z. But sometimes Z leads to A. What I mean is, I was looking for Adam, but I found Zach. Zach: You won't believe his prices. Zach: They're probably all stolen, but what you don't know won't hurt you. *Bicycles*, Zach had said. Come *on*.

I looked at his face for a long time. He hadn't been a close friend, but someone I'd known off and on for almost fifteen years, and as I looked at him I was suddenly reminded of everyone I'd known who had died of AIDS in the eighties and nineties, the tragic consequences of being in the wrong place at the wrong time. The memory was as unexpected as Adam's blow to my head but produced in me an odd, almost eerie sense of calm. Z had led to A, and A to Z, and Z back to A, but now it was a different A. History wasn't even a circle but a diminishing spiral, twisting into a tinier and tinier point.

And then:

Keith? Keith, is that you?

I didn't recognize him at first. He was shorter than I remembered, his features less fine. His eyes weren't gray but blue. But the hair was the same, thick and black and sticking out of his head in a dozen directions. It was streaked with soot now too, as if he hadn't washed in days. His T-shirt was also filthy, and pinned to his chest were three pictures that I hardly had time to take in—two women and one man, all smiling the hopelessly naive smiles of the doomed—before Adam grabbed me up in a huge embrace. His arms collapsed around me, one and then the other, and his tears salved the faded remnants of my wounded face.

Oh my god, Keith! Adam cried. You're alive!

—2004

VI.

That time you swallowed a lifesaver without sucking on it first: it stuck in your throat and when your parents heard the whistle/ wheeze coming out of you their mouths closed and all thought of their fight vanished from their faces. Black-rimmed bright circles spotted your vision, sounds came from the far end of a tunnel. You remember your father holding you upside down, smacking you on the back again and again and yelling, Is it out yet, is it out? until finally there was a pop, like a cork, and then the lifesaver was there on the floor, and your mouth tasted like cherry saliva and blood and the lifesaver was so small. And all you could think as he turned you over and pulled you close to him, wrapping his arms around your throbbing back, was, He was hitting me, he was hitting me even though he didn't want to hurt me, and you wondered if that's what he'd been doing to your mother as well.

IV

St. Anthony of the Vine

It was one of those things where everybody said they saw it coming, but no one *did* see it coming, so you have to ask yourself: were people talking to console themselves, or to make themselves feel guilty? At any rate the only one who saw it coming was me. Well, saw *her* coming. I suppose it's fair to say I was watching for her. I mean, there was a vacuum in my hand, but so much of my attention was directed out the window that the brush was zigzagging lines into the bedroom carpet like a little kid's drawing of a Christmas tree. Don't get me wrong. I didn't know *who* I was watching for, but whoever she was today, she was cutting it awful close. It was nearly four. Nicky Junger's shift out to the canning factory ended at three and it wasn't an hour back to town; Theresa left the bank at four on the nose on Thursdays—the bank was open an hour later on Thursdays—and the drive home took her twenty minutes. Thursday afternoon, three to four-twenty. Anthony called it his window of opportunity. He said he showered at Nicky's but had to be home by the time Theresa walked through the door, hair dry, half-finished kir perched precariously on the round arm of the recliner, the television tuned to *The People's Court* or *Judge Judy* and turned up just that little bit too loud. Afternoon TV's all about blame, Theresa always said, rescuing Anthony's glass with one hand and confiscating the clicker with the other—CNN to see if the world had ended and *Oprah* to see if anyone was crying about it, back to *People's Court*. You stole my country, she'd mimic, you stole my woman, you stole my car, and in one practiced gesture she'd surrender the clicker and run an index finger around Anthony's fringe of hair, and depending on how well he'd timed things that day she'd rub her finger and thumb together, or smell them, or drain his glass and walk away. That view, he said to me one time, and whistled low. That ass. Heart-shaped, even at forty-seven. All my life I have stared after women wondering what men mean by *heart-shaped*. I've found myself walking behind one or another of Anthony's women scouring their behinds for even a hint of Valentine geometry, but I have yet to come up with anything more than basic biological similarity, each to the others. But that was the thing about Anthony. Flat or fat—in back or up front—when Anthony Divine curtained up his lids to focus those Mediterranean blue eyes on a woman she always felt a little prettier than her last look in the mirror. She'd smooth her blouse over a waist a few inches skinnier than it had been a moment earlier, arch her back to accentuate a rear end no one had ever seen fit to comment on, and even if she didn't notice herself doing these things Anthony did. A woman says yes a long time before she opens her mouth, Anthony said to me another time. Locks that pesky strand of hair behind her ear, can't seem to get her bottom and top lips to meet. Just women? I'd said that time—by that time I was answering him back. Men are impervious to the female gaze? Oh come on Mira, Anthony drawled, don't get your skirt in a twist. When have you ever known a man to say no?

LIKE I SAID: I was watching for her, but I still managed to miss the moment she stepped outside. By the time I made it to the kitchen window she was halfway down Nicky Junger's sidewalk, and all I could see was a cotton-candy mass that seemed to have swallowed her head. Good lord, girl, I thought when I saw that rat's nest, pull a comb through that mane, you want everyone in town to know you been on your back? And: Good lord, Anthony, I thought as well, does she always have to be *blond*? This one's hair was such a fright I couldn't get a clear view of her face, and at first it looked like I wasn't going to because she headed straight down the sidewalk instead of cutting across Nicky Junger's patch of lawn to mine. There was a car parked on Front Court, one of those silver bubble–type things, and I thought she was going to take herself on home and fix herself there. He didn't always send them to me. But then I saw there was something wrong with the way she was walking. Short jerky steps, one foot swinging out wide before landing directly in front of the other, like a gymnast learning the balance beam. And as I'm sure you know it was the middle of March but Nicky Junger's raggedy lawn already needed mowing, which is why it took me a moment to see that today's victim only had the one shoe on, a wooden-soled Candie with enough of a heel to carousel her body up and down as she made her way to the street, her hands clutched to her stomach and her back so bent I wondered if maybe he'd punched her. But then she reached the street and turned away from her car, turned toward my trailer, and I saw it was worse than all that. I saw it was Kennedy Albright this time, and I saw the blood on the front of her sweater. I had to move to the dining room to keep her in sight. I dropped the vacuum and squeezed around the table, but I kept my eyes on her. On her legs, swinging in wide arcs to accommodate the ample flesh of her thighs and that one elevated foot, and on her second shoe, heelless, dangling from her hands in front of her stomach, its slope paralleling the wet red stain on her sweater like a pair of stockings hung from a mantel. Behind me the abandoned vacuum chewed up a single square of carpet as, zombielike, Kennedy advanced on my trailer. There was a disconnect there, Kennedy's silent lopsided progress down Front Court and the deafening whine inside my trailer, which is maybe why I could suddenly hear Anthony saying, It's a difference Mira, between people who call what they live in a home and who call it a trailer. Said it, I remembered, only after he'd moved out of his own tin shell around the corner from me on Back Court. *Trailer*'s such a hopeless word, he said when he no longer lived in one, something left over, left behind. The word, I said, or the thing? I waved his answer away before he could give it. The residents of the Borderlands Trailer Court *are* left behinds, I said. Left behind by life or leaving something behind, take your pick. Certainly no one had left behind more than Anthony Divine. His hair for one thing—just that gray fringe wreathing his sun-browned skull like dried-up laurel—and, too, Linda Diego said there wasn't nothing but three suitcases in the trunk of the gray Cadillac he parked in front of the trailer court office. A matched set, was all Linda Diego said about Anthony's suitcases, each bigger than the last. When she showed him round to Lot 17 Back Court, she said he took all three of those suitcases out and stacked them one on top of the other, smallest to largest, like one of them ziggurats in the desert that Cardo, my daughter's husband, took pictures of when he was in Iraq, but upside down. Linda Diego said the suitcases were made of rich brown leather and even stacked up like that, inverted, precarious, they still seemed more solid than the trailer she showed him into, leaving me to wonder, among other things, if Linda Diego wasn't the first—the first in Saches, I mean. Eyes like . . . like blue things, Linda Diego said, and thanks to her I knew to be on guard against them the first time Anthony Divine strolled into the café and ordered a bowl of tomato soup and turned in the diamond on his pinkie ring before picking up his spoon, and after he left I found myself wondering what the fuss was about. It was only later on that I realized he hadn't bothered to show them to me. His eyes, I mean. Like he said: a woman says no a long time before she opens her mouth.

I WAS STANDING in the open door by the time Kennedy Albright staggered up the steps but she pressed the doorbell anyway. She used the loose red heel of her broken shoe to stab the button, and what with the door open the bell's buzz was loud enough to make her and me both jump—I'd shut the vacuum off by then, though too late to save that particular square of carpet. Kennedy Albright's hands hung in front of the oozing stain on her sweater, limp helpless things like the front paws of a rabbit standing up on its hind legs. The tips of her fingers were red too, and their jangly-spoked spread made it look like she was knitting the stain out of her blood like a sock. But there was still a connection I wasn't making, the stain on her sweater, the stained splintered heel, and this was what finally drove me to speak. Honey? I said. Kennedy, baby, what happened? There was the same flush to her cheeks that all of them had when he finished with them, in some ways the faraway look in her eyes was the same too, but there was also a long scratch along her jaw and her eyes were looking to another place. Did he fuck her first? I wondered then, surprising myself with the ugliness of the word, which I'd never consciously applied to what Anthony did to the women he took to Nicky Junger's trailer. But now I had to wonder, did he actually fuck her before he did whatever he did that cut her jaw open and . . . and stained her sweater? But even as Kennedy looked up at me I saw two things: saw first of all that it wasn't her blood on her sweater, and saw, over her shoulder, coming down Front Court, Nicky Junger's car heading for her driveway. My god, Mira, Kennedy said again, but even that was what they all said, tottering up the stairs, one hand on the small of their back, My god, and I clung to that. I held on to the familiarity of the words, the safety of them. *There will be a rational explanation for all of this* is what I was telling myself, but Kennedy was still talking. Theresa's gonna kill me when she finds out, she said, picking at the edges of the stain on her sweater as though it were a sticker she could peel off, and when Nicky Junger started screaming Kennedy looked up and over my head as if a bird was calling out, or an angel. My sister's husband, Kennedy said after Nicky finally stopped screaming. My god. She touched the cut on her chin and stared at the reddened fingertip and then, frowning, licked it clean, and when she looked at the red-tipped heel in her hand I almost thought she was going to lick that too, but all she did was shake it from her fingers, not in horror or even in surprise, but like it was a sticky candy wrapper she had to flick away to get off her skin. The shoe fell between two of the loose cinder blocks that make up my porch. A genuine Candie, not some retro knockoff. Thirty years out of style that shoe must've been, just like Kennedy's beehive. The police had to take my whole porch apart to find it there among the spiders' nests and mulching leaves and a Visa bill from July 1998, and they never did put it back together. Cardo built that porch on one of their trips down from Dallas, and he promised that when they came for Thanksgiving he'd rebuild it but until then I had to climb in and out of my trailer on one up-ended block, making sure not to trip on the police tape: CRIME SCENE DO NOT CROSS. But that was all in the future. Just then it was still the stain on Kennedy's sweater, and Anthony's eyes. He wouldn't even look at me, Mira, is the last thing Kennedy said before she came inside, he couldn't be bothered, and if it's true what she said, that that's when I invited her in—I honestly don't remember—then it's because I understood what she meant, if not what had happened. I understood her because of the afternoon Anthony took his first midday meal at the café. Am I too late for lunch? he'd said that day, and in fact it was two-thirty, which is to say shift-change time. He'd been in a few times before, like I said, tomato soup to stay or Earl Grey to go—not a trailer, Mira, a home—but now it was shift-change time, and it was his future wife herself who said, What're you trying to do, Anthony, maximize your waitress potential? Said it to him the very first time he sat at her table, which was his second day in a row in the café: you could accuse Anthony of a lot of things but you could never accuse him of not knowing what he wanted. Anthony smiled at Theresa without looking up, but he managed to catch her hand in his when he intercepted the cup of coffee Theresa was aiming for the table. I saw her wince a little as the turned-in diamond of Anthony's pinkie ring pressed into her flesh, and then I saw, for the first time, Anthony's eyes, and I realized I'd been guarding myself against an attack that hadn't come. The lids didn't lift as much as fold into each other, fifty-some-odd years of squint wrinkles closing in upon themselves like what they call Roman blinds, and then, glowing slightly, the palest blue eyes I have ever seen lit up the restaurant. Eyes that seemed innocent as water flowing under ice and experienced as a thousand-year-old harbor, eyes as full of potential as a wishing well. Eyes you could believe in. Anthony wasn't even looking at me and still I found myself wanting to believe in him. *Potential*, is the first word anyone ever heard Anthony Divine say to Theresa Blanchette. Now that's got a nice sound to it. Even before Theresa got back to the waitress station she was stage-whispering, My *god*, Mira, but if Anthony heard her he didn't look up. Did you *see* that, Mira? Theresa said to me. I seen it before, I said. I'll see it again. But what I was thinking was, No. No I have never seen nothing like that in my life. I haven't seen it because he couldn't be bothered to show it to me. The impudent son of a—Theresa was still saying. I am a *married woman*. But then, married or single, shift change or swollen ankles—Rolanda Ezquivel was at that very moment rolling up her knee-highs in the stockroom—Theresa grabbed the coffeepot and marched straight back to Anthony's table. Refill, Mr. Divine? she called out, and Anthony said, Not *Divine* actually. *De-Vine*. As in, of the vine. St. Anthony of the Vine, Theresa said, though where the first word came from is anybody's guess. Well Mr. De-Vine, my name is Theresa Blan-chette. As in Jock Blanchette, my *husband*. Can't say I've made his acquaintance, Anthony said without looking up, at which point Theresa pivoted on her heel and marched back to me one more time, her cheeks diaper-rash red. Did you ever? Mira? Did you? Many times, I said, but I was looking at myself in the mirror behind the dessert rack, wondering what Theresa had that I didn't, besides Angie Dickinson's hair dye. Why, Mira Beller, Theresa interrupted my reverie. I do believe you doubt my integrity. Theresa, I said then, taking the pot from her and putting it back on the burner. He didn't order coffee. He ordered a bowl of tomato soup. He only ever orders a bowl of tomato soup or a cup of Earl Grey tea. *To go.*

THERE ARE SOME experiences that only make sense while they're happening, others that don't add up till they're over and done with. I remember waking up to a quiet house the morning after my daughter married Ricardo and thinking, So this is what it's all about. You raise them up to let them go. With Harney it was the other way around. He's been gone more than a decade now, and with each passing day he feels more and more like something I dreamed up. The feelings he stroked from me are vague and prickly like the clotted air around the power station, and sometimes, at the strangest times—when I'm washing dishes, say, or when I'm sitting in the middle of Fifth and Encenada waiting to make a left-hand turn—a hot wave of him washes over my skin and I feel embarrassed, as if someone had caught me in public with my hand in my drawers. With Theresa it was like my daughter. I tried starting a pool among the waitresses as to when she'd cave, just a joke you understand, I myself didn't think she *would* cave, but before the first date came up Anthony'd already dragged her into his cave by her hair. Whereas with Kennedy it was like it was with Harney. I don't actually remember inviting her in, don't remember locking the door or serving her coffee. The coffee, I know, was already made—I always had a pot going by two-thirty, three o'clock on Thursdays—but who poured I couldn't tell you, and for all I know she called the police on herself. At any rate it was she who unlocked the door and let them in. What I do remember her saying was that it wasn't the heel of her shoe that killed him. She said she hadn't broken off her heel in his ribs until she stamped on his prostrate body. St. Anthony of the Vine, the martyrdom of: he served her the glass of wine he always served them after they finished, but Kennedy dropped hers, it was an accident, she stressed, but she still managed to spill wine down the front of Anthony's shirt and break Nicky Junger's glass. She stained Nicky's carpet too, a little archipelago of purple blobs that people tend not to notice, Nicky told me later, next to the continental smear of Anthony's lifeblood, but it was still only the spilled wine Kennedy was concerned with when Anthony called her a bitch—the spilled wine and of course the broken glass. She was just standing up with a few of the larger pieces in her hand when Anthony called her a clumsy little bitch and slapped her, cutting her cheek with the turned-in diamond on his pinkie ring, and depending on whose account you believe it was either accidentally or on purpose that the stem of Nicky Junger's broken wine glass penetrated Anthony's throat when Kennedy slapped him back. He wouldn't even look at me, Kennedy said right before the police took her away, but I just shook my head. Mira, Kennedy said then, you don't think I'd intentionally kill my own sister's husband, do you? To which the prosecuting attorney later replied, You wouldn't think she'd sleep with him either. And even I have to admit it's hard to escape the idea of hostile intent when you look at those pictures of Anthony with the circular dimpled base of a wine glass filling the hollow of his throat looking for all the world like a suction cup, you know, the kind you use to stick a mirror to shower-stall mylar or a sign in your rear window. IF YOU CAN READ THIS YOU'RE TOO DAMN CLOSE! Pottery Barn, eleven ninety-five, Nicky Junger said in response to the prosecutor's question, and she even held up an unbroken glass so that the nine men and three women of the jury could see the full two and a half inches of stem that Kennedy Albright had buried in Anthony's throat. Nicky told me a gasp went through the courtroom when she produced that glass—said she herself convicted Kennedy when, pinkie ring or no pinkie ring, disfiguring scar or little old scratch on her cheek, she tried to balance Anthony's slap against Kennedy's retaliatory gesture. But Nicky, I argued with her, think who was slapping her. He wasn't a saint, he married her sister. Correction, Nicky said. Theresa married *him*—the fool. Which, I have to admit, is what I myself called Theresa the Wednesday after the Tuesday she missed her third shift in two weeks. I drove down to Monterrey yesterday, was all Theresa said, and even though Monterrey isn't exactly down from Saches—in the same way Saches isn't exactly down from Dallas—all I said was, Why on earth didn't you call in first? I believe they call it a Monterrey divorce, is what Theresa said. Or do they just call it a Mexican divorce? Well, I told her I was firing her for skipping out on yet another shift but if I'm being honest I was really firing her for being a fool. Theresa Blanchette, is what I told her, you are the biggest fool on either side of the border, but she only shook her head. Theresa DeVine now, she said. She dropped her nametag on the counter, twisted her new ring on her finger, faded letters on a sticky label replaced by a loop of beaten gold. We got us a Mexican wedding too. In the months to come— by which I mean in the months before Anthony got around to seducing his wife's sister—that last gesture of Theresa's haunted me. She twisted that ring on her finger as though the marriage it stood for were as solid as its circle, without beginning, end, or interruption. But there's a difference between a ring and a marriage, a thing and the idea of it. An idea isn't a sprung coil of facts, it's just an equation measuring the space between the world and the words that float around it. Meaning's always a relationship. X is X because of its distance from Y, but also because of how close it is to Z. And while we're at it, tell me this: why is it always X, Y, and Z or A, B, and C? Why always the first or last three letters of the alphabet? Another example: the relationship of my grandsons (Fowler, Ferris, and Rodrigo, a triumvirate typical of a border town, even if their parents live in Dallas now) to my homemade apple pie. It's significantly altered if I serve that pie with store-bought ice cream, which is to say that if I serve it alone they leave half on their plates but if I pile enough Ben and Jerry's on it they eat it all. Which says, I know, something about my pie, but also says something about my grandsons and how their parents are raising them. My maternal grandmother was a terrible cook too— gingersnaps are what she made when I came over, and you could've shingled a chicken coop with them. But I'd've never dreamed of leaving the table without cleaning up everything she'd taken the time to prepare for me. Which is why—to return to my original point—Theresa's gesture with the ring stuck with me. Because call it what you will, Mexican wedding, or *boda*, or Act II in the tragedy of St. Anthony of the Vine, it wasn't two months after Theresa and Anthony went down to Monterrey that Anthony was back in the café, alone. It was around ten. Another in-between time, the breakfast crowd gone but too early for lunch, so that when Anthony strolled through the door the place was empty except for Alvin Porterhouse and Edgar Taylor smoking their tenth or eleventh one-last-cigarette-before-we-head-out. Anthony sat at the counter instead of his usual booth but he ordered tomato soup same as always, and I kind of kept one eye on him as I prepped for lunch, but all he did was stare down into his bowl. Then I heard the bells tinkle as Alvin and Edgar finally headed out and more or less on cue Anthony said, Can I interest you in a proposition, Mira? All at once I saw those eyes I'd seen focused on Theresa—the eyes that had looked like wishing wells to me— and even though my hair was all wound up in a hairnet I still found myself patting it in place. Why, Anthony, I said, turning, but he was still staring into his soup bowl. Theresa's got herself a job at First National, he said. Telling. She's a teller, I mean. Teller's hours. By now I was standing in front of him and those eyes made it as far up as my navel, which despite myself I was sucking as flat as I could, but when Anthony said, I'd like to use your trailer if I could, I let it pooch out over my apron. You ought to be ashamed of yourself, I said. You ain't but six weeks married. Seven, Anthony said. He didn't take his eyes off my stomach. I told her, he said. What did you tell her? I told her who I was, Anthony said. Anthony, I demanded, but then I broke off. Why don't you ever *look at me* when I'm talking to you! Anthony let go of his spoon then. He put the hand that had held it on his forehead. At first he just rubbed the dome of his head, smooth and spotted above his tufted fringe, and then he tilted his head back and managed to lift up his lids as far as my mouth maybe, or my nose, but then his eyes fell all the way back to the counter. But still there had been that blue, the blue of the earth seen from the moon. There had been two of them, the world and its twin. Ocular myasthenia gravis, Anthony said. Do what? I said. You asked me why I don't look at you. I have a condition called ocular myasthenia gravis. The muscles in my eyelids are failing. In a few more years I won't be able to open them at all. Anthony, I—I shook my head. Why did you bother to marry her? Anthony shrugged. Women are as different as countries, he said. It takes a different strategy to conquer each one. Marriage is what it took to get Theresa. And do you know what? I took him at his word. I believed him is what I'm saying. I bought his explanation for why he'd married Theresa even as I knew that occult Mayan Indian gravies—it wasn't until later on I looked it up, I wanted to get it right at the trial—was just a polite way of saying I wasn't worth the effort, and perhaps I let him get away with the whole conquering countries line because, despite myself, I was hurt that he hadn't tried to invade me. But I still wouldn't let him use my trailer for his trysts. That it turned out to be Nicky Junger who did struck me at first as just my bad luck—I was over the hill and not worth climbing, but every Thursday I got the privilege of looking out my window at greener pastures. But then he started sending them over. A woman wants to chat, he told me the day after someone who called herself

Raylene Daylong had knocked on my trailer door. I figure they can talk to you as much as me. Of course I knew why he was sending them to me—and it wasn't what he told them, so he could clean up Nicky's place before she got back. He sent them to me in lieu of himself. A token of what had been withheld. An apology even, almost. He wanted me to know I was still good for something, and for my part I accepted his once-a-week surrogate into my house, be she barely out of high school or middle-aged and freshly dyed. Every Thursday after I got home from the café I vacuumed and made a pot of coffee and let some flush-faced floozy sit at my kitchen table and reapply her lipstick. Their talk was frank— loose, I want to say, but that's probably just jealousy. At any rate Anthony's women used words in my trailer they'd've never used in their own homes, until at some point they realized I wasn't a fellow traveler and then, cheeks freshly reddened with modesty— embarrassment, I want to say, shame—they would take their leave, and after they left I washed their lipstick off my cups in the same way Anthony must have washed it from his mouth. But the only time I saw the man himself was in the café, pinkie ring on one hand and wedding ring on the other. He always turned his pinkie ring in before he started eating but his wedding ring he let hang any which way on his thin finger, crooked, lopsided, a hoop tossed at the fair that just barely manages to lasso its pylon. What was it they saw in him? A skinny bald man with lazy eyes pushing sixty. His lids were so tired that he ate his soup with his eyes closed, spattering the counter and sometimes his shirt with red drops it's hard not to see as harbingers of his fate, and only when he paid did he look at my apron, at my hand passing him his change.

Ocular myasthenia gravis may have explained that but it didn't explain why the man could say *It's you* to a different woman every week and be believed every time. A man who, six months buried in the cemetery behind Our Lady of Sorrows, still had the occasional female caller knocking on Nicky Junger's door come Thursday afternoon. It was the one point missed by every story Rolanda Ezquivel clipped from the Dallas papers for me (witnesses weren't allowed to read about the case while it was going on): that he didn't conquer these women as much as they invited him in. In fact it was an old-fashioned gladiator match, that trial, the stories written about it: everyone a victim but no one innocent. You could have your blood and drink it too. But that's what happens when a personal tragedy explodes into the world. The people disappear and there are only plotlines left, equations, X and Y and Z, A and B and C, until history moves on and then what's left? Nothing. Nothing but words and pictures. At forty-seven Kennedy Albright had somehow been cast as the innocent girl pushed beyond her comprehension by an experienced seducer, in direct contrast to her older sister, an aged fleshy former beauty queen (by which they seemed to mean Winter Homecoming 1971) who thought she could trade up at the end of her life. At any rate that's what the prosecutor said. Love, the prosecutor said, like life itself, starts to die the moment it's born. That's why love, he went on, like life itself, requires institutions to sustain it, nurture it through the long years of its senescence. We call those institutions marriage and the state. Both are fraught, both compromises that sacrifice freedom's anarchy in the interests of stability. Marriage's yoke hardens its team while ensuring they seam a single track. The state's grasp on its citizens is more convulsive, now light, now nearly crushing. Citizens of the state of Texas and of this great country, the prosecutor said, we are here today to ensure that Kennedy Albright does not wiggle out of justice's grip. By exiling her from the state you will be protecting and strengthening what remains, so that perhaps Theresa Albright Blanchette DeVine can reclaim her place among self-respecting law-abiding citizens. To which the defense replied, It wasn't *my* client who first mocked the institution of marriage: it was yours. Which answer didn't keep Kennedy out of jail but at least saved her life. Or at least that was Cardo's take on the whole thing. Mami, he said that Christmas—they hadn't been able to make it down for Thanksgiving after all—calm down. It's not like he means what he says. He's speaking to a higher purpose: conviction. Am I the only one who sees the contradiction in that? I said. That the law has to betray its *convictions* in order to secure a *conviction*? Give it a rest, Mami. You think too much, you hurt your brain. I'm going to go fix up your porch now. But Cardo, I said, following him, what's the difference between the stories the prosecutor told and the stories Anthony told? How long is it before people lose their faith in the institution of law just like Kennedy lost her faith in Anthony? I think someone's projecting a little, Cardo said. Ay, Mami, he went on, hauling the scattered cinderblocks of my porch to one side, only in America would an old man's exuberance lead to talk of revolution. I stood in the elevated doorway and looked down at Cardo's white-shirted back, beginning to dot with sweat as he dragged the blocks out of the way. Exuberance? Cardo, he called them *countries*. He said he had to *conquer* them. And he was good as his word, wasn't he? Cardo said, raking smooth the mangy patch of dirt below my door. Words want to be true, he went on, and people want them to be true. He set his rake down and reached for the first block and said, If they don't start out true then people tend to make them true, and then he laid the block with a thud in the soft earth. All I'm asking, Cardo, is for a little honesty, in love, in law. In life. Cardo edged one block next to another, three wide, three deep. Where's the fun in that? he said, his voice distant, distracted by the effort of aligning the blocks. Who's talking about fun, Cardo? Mami, Cardo interrupted me as he laid the first block of the second tier heavily on the base, listen to me. The block made a dry scraping noise as he slid it into place. Once upon a time your Texas was part of my country, Cardo said. Your California, your Arizona, your Nuevo México were all a part of *viejo* Mexico. You like the old country so much, Cardo, why not move back? *Listen*, Mami, Cardo said, smacking the second-tier blocks in place faster than he had the first, one up against the others, three across, two deep, leaving a block-wide step. There is a reason why your side won. A reason why there is no INS in Mexico, no border guards to keep the Americans out, no dogs sniffing their pockets for drugs. A channel of sweat ran down his back now as, grunting, he lifted the first block of the third tier and let it fall in place just a few inches below my feet. What're you saying, Cardo, that might makes right? To the victor belongs the spoils? That Anthony got what he deserved? I couldn't resist adding, even though it didn't quite follow. All I'm saying, Cardo panted, hauling the second block of the third tier over, is that your grandsons wear shoes instead of making them in a factory outside Oaxaca.

There was one block left and Cardo turned for it with a sigh. I'm saying that your daughter's skin is too fair for the Chihuahua sun, he said, pushing the block wearily into place, and then he wiped the sweat from his forehead and smeared a little dirt in its place. I love Mexico is what I'm saying, he said finally, squinting up at me, but for my wife's sake, my children's, I live in the U.S. of A., because your greedy gringo government lets me provide for my family in a way that my poncho-wearing *presidente* does not. *Hmph*, I sniffed. Your children won't even eat my apple pie. I see them once, maybe twice a year, and they won't even eat my apple pie. Cardo just shook his head then, held one hand up to me. C'mon, Mami, let's go pick your finicky American grandsons up from the park and buy them ice cream. When we get back I'll see what I can do about your carpet. I had to think for a moment, then I remembered: the shag strands had gotten tangled in the vacuum's rollers and I'd had to hack them out with a knife. It seemed to me that my efforts to tell Cardo the story of St. Anthony of the Vine had been similarly crude, a rescue operation that lost as much as it saved. I make the pies myself, I said now. Homemade, I said, but then I remembered Anthony's words. Trailer-made, I said, but Cardo just shook his head. They like ice cream, he said. Give them what they like, they eat it all. Now come on, you know how your daughter hates to be kept waiting. But still I hung back. I pointed to the porch. Shouldn't you test it first? Mami, it's fine. It's cinderblock, it's not going nowhere, let's go. I looked down at the blocks. Yesterday they'd been too heavy for me to lift but today I doubted they would hold my weight. I wanted an assurance that these blocks would be more concrete than ocular myasthenia gravis, a proof against sorrow, not the cause of it. Cardo, I said, I can hardly afford a broken hip at my age. Mami, Cardo said. For seven months you climbed in and out of your house on one wobbly block. What is this about? Cardo, I said then, he wouldn't even look at me. He couldn't be bothered. And Cardo. Sweet Cardo. He'd built his three-tiered pyramid two times, he could build it a thousand times and every time it would come out the same, and now he ascended it like a gold medalist climbing to the topmost platform and looked right at me with eyes the color of the soil his rebuilt porch stood upon. Mami, my son-in-law said, and he put one of his hands right on top of my breast. He only won those women because they were already lost. He knocked on my ribs with a hand callused from years of honest labor and gritty besides, from the work he'd done for me. Love like that is a dictator, Cardo said, still staring me in the eye, but you are already empress of your own heart.

Ricardo looked at me until I dropped my head on his warm damp shirt, and then *Viva Zapatista*, he murmured as I cried into his shoulder. Long live the revolution.

—2008

VII.

This much you remember: the light, beside the bed. It was thin, and it hid the color of his hair. You know his hair was—what color was his hair? Blond? Black? Was it brown, like yours? In your memory of that night it has no tint save that of the light that cupped it as though it were leaves—mint, chamomile, elder-flower, rosehips. Anodyne soporifics, but amnesia's cold comfort to one left alone. You'd take any color, fair or dark, any length, as long as it grew from his head. You'd even take a wig if it was him it capped, rather than a phantom of memory that holds your soul trapped in its own dreams, delusions, fantasies, fictions. Even now, thinking about him, the image is so nebulous that he could be thinking up you, the brush that draws the hand that holds it, the painting that dreams the man. Nouns are naming words, he told you once. Verbs are fluid, he said, nouns frozen. Names are power, he said. That may be, you countered, but verbs are revolution. He told you that everything he's ever written has come, in some way, from his life, and sometimes he feels there will never be enough exciting moments for him to finish even this one book. And once he told you, right before he fucked you, that language is just a way to measure loss. Later, when you said his name aloud, you found that, indeed, it had no meaning. You spoke again: It's me, you said. More empty words. After that you learned to keep quiet.

Summer Beam, pt. 1

The signs popped into Ellen's head right after she got on 90. It was just outside of Albany, where Nathan usually launched into the second round of his rant against weekends at Popham Beach. The first installment would've come as soon as she'd backed out of the driveway in Saratoga. She couldn't *possibly* expect him to drive for six hours in the dark, could she? He had *night blindness*, she *knew* that, although this condition didn't prevent him from reading an entire novel by the glove compartment's little light. After eight years the routine had become so familiar that even though Nathan wasn't in the car Ellen still found herself arguing with him in her head. It's *ridiculous*, she could hear him whining, we drive thirty miles south to go fifty miles north. We spend half the weekend in the goddamned car! The complaints were always the same, only the book changed: Dorothy Sayers or Patricia Highsmith or one of those other "lady detectrix sleuth-sayers" from the last century. And this *road*, she remembered him saying—last year? the year before? She couldn't remember the date but she'd never forget the prissy way he'd turned a page, as if neither wife nor novel was worth the full measure of his attention. It has almost as many peaks and valleys as Miss Sayers's—how shall I put it?—*crenellated* narrative. And he'd flipped another page he couldn't possibly have read, tamped fussily on the stack of superannuated roadmaps in the glove compartment in an attempt to get more light to shine on *Strong Poison* or *Gaudy Night* and then, wheezing—why were these Samsungs so *heavy?*—pulled out his phone and propped it above his book, the screen's glow illuminating the lines of text like a UFO hovering over a cornfield.

Ellen would try to remain calm. Would remind Nathan that even with the detour south the interstate knocked more than an hour off the trip; would tell him that if he thought the Mass Pike was torturous he should try the glorified deer paths laid over the mountains of Vermont and New Hampshire like so many snippets of ribbon fallen from a seamstress's scissors. She'd said all this—not for the first time but, it now seemed, the last—could it really have been two years ago? Three? When *was* the last time she'd talked Nathan into going to her family's beach house?

As if in answer, a campaign poster popped into her head. It hadn't really been a poster at all, just an 11 x 17 placard taped to a metal post on the edge of the road's shoulder, thin cardstock flapping like a snared bird's wings as they sped past. BARACK OBAMA. CHANGE WE CAN BELIEVE IN. Although leave it to Nathan to have a different take: It looks like one of those memorials, he'd said the last time they drove up. You know, the smiling photograph of the deceased, the line of sentimental verse. All it needs is a few plastic flowers and you've got democracy's tombstone right there. Ellen had thought Nathan was reaching (she thought that of most of his criticism), but had given him the benefit of the doubt and glanced in the rearview mirror. But it had been too dark to see the sign—too dark to see anything, in fact, and for a moment she had the vertiginous feeling that they'd left the road behind, the planet, and were hurtling through the void of space. But no, that was just their marriage.

And then the CHANGE WE CAN BELIEVE IN poster disappeared from her memory, replaced by the faded KEEP OF THE GRASS! signs in the dunes behind the Popham Beach house—by, more specifically, the fear that someone had finally pulled them down during her protracted absence. Could it really have been three years? The thought so plagued her that she had to throw her phone in the backseat to keep from calling her mother, and, five hours later, when she finally made it to the house, she rushed from the car, pulled the key from the mailbox, wound her way through the shadowy maze of furniture in the tiny living room to the double doors at the back of the house, throwing them open like the spurned woman in pretty much every opera she knew, and—

And nothing. It was as if the blackness she'd seen in the rear-view mirror three years ago had been magnified a thousand times, a million. The darkness was so complete, so pervasive, that despite her grip on the door handles she felt that the world had ceased to exist. Moon and stars seemed every bit as improbable as the layer of cloud that the rational part of her brain knew was hiding them from view. She couldn't even bring herself to step onto the deck, as if it too might have slipped away without the sun's sentry light to keep it in check. All she could do was stand there, bewildered and exhilarated, as much at her reaction as at the darkness.

And then the sound of the surf pushed its way through her ears; the smell of salt; the cutaneous prickle of moisture-laden air, like static electricity pulling on the hairs of her arms, but cold. With each familiar sensation Ellen relaxed, and after a moment she took a step backward, pulled the doors closed, turned from the darkness as if it were nothing more than a black curtain behind which a stage was being set. Went upstairs, fell onto her unmade bed; and when she came back down three or four hours later (she didn't know what time it was, or what time she'd gotten in for that matter) the sun was up and the signs were waiting in the dunes as she knew they would be. Because that's what Popham Beach was. The place where nothing changed.

In fact she'd forgotten about them while she slept. Had come out on the back deck with a cup of coffee not to check on the signs' persistence but because that's what you did your first morning in Popham Beach: you made a cup of coffee and walked out onto the deck to sip it in the presence of the ocean—and there they were, pinned to the four corners of the Baldwin property as though it were a beach blanket that needed to be secured at the edges. The wet patch of grass they staked out was silvered like an old woman's hair, the sand visible between the coarse strands flaky as a dandruffy scalp. The impression was of disheveledness, age, even weakness, but the signs she'd painted the summer between second and third grades served as a faint but firm reminder of the conservationist lesson her mother had taught her thirty-one years ago: that this tiny patch of grass and sand was all that stood between the omnivorous waves pounding the beach and the moss-edged shakes of the little house at her back. Half a mile north a dramatic stand of hoodoos testified to the waves' power, the jagged pockmarked columns resembling a bombed-out city, right down to the wire and pipe tangled around their bases, the splintered rafters, the shattered glass. The Baldwin house was the last left on this stretch of 18. Her parents had bought in '68, when Jackie was two, and over the course of four decades six neighbors had lost their homes, while the original Popham Colony (founded in 1607, the same year as its more famous rival in Jamestown) was now almost a quarter mile offshore and twenty feet underwater. A whole shelf in her father's study in Worcester was given over to bits of clay- and stoneware that still sometimes washed up on the beach, including a bone-white kaolin pipe with a stem as long and thin as a heron's femur, remarkably unbroken despite the four centuries it had spent beneath the waves.

But for now the only thing the crashing surf obliterated was the sound of NPR at her back. A brisk breeze swirled loose grains of sand over Ellen's bare feet but the steaming cup in her hands balanced out the chill. Well, physically anyway: she hadn't stopped for coffee at the minimart in Brunswick last night. Hadn't wanted to suffer the stare of some pimply sixteen-year-old at her mascara-scarred cheeks or field the presumptuous questions of a cigarette-smelling divorcée about what brought her here in the off-season—and at this hour too! And so the cup in her hands was decaf, and stale, a relic of Jackie's third pregnancy, when, in addition to alcohol and tobacco, she'd given up caffeine, sugar, red meat, and—the kicker in a family whose nominal Catholicism manifested itself in Friday night spaghetti fests observed with Lenten stringency—the entire family of deadly nightshades. At any rate, Cooper would be five in the new year, and Ellen had had to scrape half an inch of permafrost off the top of Jackie's coffee to yield a few useable if symbolic spoonfuls.

Not that she could have expected any better. After four decades her mother had become adept at eating down the staples, so that when she shut the house at Labor Day the cabinets were bare of perishables, and just about everything else. When Ellen looked for coffee this morning she found three half-empty bottles of olive oil, four different kinds of vinegar, two boxes of kosher salt; she also found two cans of cat food, which was odd, since the Baldwins didn't have a cat. The sea air had rendered the boxes of salt hard as bricks inside their cardboard casing—but it was the smell of that same wet air that had filled Ellen's nostrils as she sat in the car last night after Nathan made his announcement. The ocean, she'd thought. Seagulls and sea shells; cormorants and knobby tangles of kelp; watery dawns flooding her family's 182-year-old cottage with umber waves of light. Above all, the smells: brine, fish, the ineffable algid damp. The remembered odor had drawn Ellen all the way across Massachusetts and up the Maine coast like a bear in a cartoon following a ribbon of scent, and the reality hadn't let her down—although it was tempered by another smell, sharp, unpleasant: a dead horseshoe crab probably, or one of those seabirds that ominously dropped out of the sky every few months.

But it was the grass that provided her first measure of solace this morning. The signs. KEEP OF THE GRASS! The optimism—the blind trust!—in their diligently repeated misspelling spoke to what her father unironically called the core Baldwin belief, namely, that the present could only be understood through its relationship to past and future. We owe a debt to one and a responsibility to the other, he'd said more times than the Baldwin children could count (even if the debt and the responsibility changed places with almost every iteration). "The emperors of Rome preserved peace by a constant preparation for war" was (according to him anyway) another way of saying the same thing. He'd said this to Nathan once, identified it as a line from Gibbon, but Nathan had one-upped him, told her father that Gibbon got it from someone called Vegetius. *Si vis pacem, para bellum*: "If you want peace, prepare for war." Ellen, clueless how to handle a conflict between her husband and her father, had done the first thing that popped into her head: she put her foot on Nathan's crotch under the table, and been surprised—but then, on reflection, not—to find him already erect.

She smiled at the memory, one of the few pleasant ones involving Nathan and Popham Beach, held her cup to her chin and breathed in the idea of caffeine and let herself take comfort in the insulating emptiness of a house full of fond memories but, mercifully, lacking a telephone line. There was the cell, of course, its bloc of stored family data waiting on the floor of the car. Three numbers each for Jackie and Paul (home, work, cell), home and cell for Mom, work and cell for Dad, a bulwark laid out like the Slavic states between Ellen's private and public domains. Though Ellen, the youngest, was now thirty-eight, the Baldwins remained a close-knit unit. When she took the job at Skidmore ten years ago—she taught her first class the week before 9/11, so it was easy to remember—she'd pledged to spend every other weekend at Popham Beach; and when, the following spring, Nathan accompanied her on the very first trip, it seemed like some key piece of the generational puzzle had fallen into place. Jackie had William, Paul Lane, and now she had Nathan. The frame had been completed, all they had to do was fill in the details. In many ways the invitation to Popham Beach was more important than the wedding (held a year later at the beach house, as had been Paul's and Jackie's). In true Baldwin fashion, Nathan's presence had been treated as a purely logistical issue: the twin bed in Ellen's room had been replaced with a full, and that was that; and when she started coming on her own, Nathan's absence was similarly unremarked upon (the bed, however, remained). Even so, she found herself making up excuses as thin as the ones her students came up with. Nathan had a sore throat, he had computer trouble, he was on deadline, he was at a conference. One time she'd even said he had to stay home to take care of a dog they didn't own. We're dog-sitting, she'd said, though no one had asked when they got a dog. When she could no longer face her mother and Jackie's double-barreled silence, she made one last-ditch effort to get him to come up with her, after which they both stopped going.

That had been three years ago, if the Obama memory was correct. Hard to believe it'd been so long. The thousands of meals and hundreds of classes and . . . and what else had she done during the past three years? It was all blurry—all a darkness, she wanted to say, like the narrator of *The Good Soldier*, then pushed that thought into the maudlin pile.

But that final disastrous drive was as fresh in her mind as if they'd come up last weekend. I mean, *divided highway*, she could hear Nathan saying as clearly as if he were on the deck with her. Aspirated voice indicating air quotes, deep breath presaging a lecture on the—would it be Orwellian this time? Chomskyan? Žižekian?—relationship of bureaucracy to language. I mean, it's an oxymoron, isn't it? Roads are supposed to *connect* things, not divide them. It's as if the failure of this particular motorway to get you to your destination mirrors—manifests—an existential failing. It's not just that it can't get you there: it doesn't *want* to. The little quaver in his voice, as if he knew that she knew that he was reaching—was, if you wanted to get right down to it, conflating the participial *divided* with *divisive*, which shared an etymological root but wasn't an inflection of *divide* (if you were going to call out Dr. Nathan Miller, PhD, you damn well better be ready to back up your claim). But all Ellen said was: The *joke* is about *park*ways and *drive*ways. What—Why do we *drive* on the *park*way and *park* in the *drive*way. That's the *joke*. Nathan *hmmm*ed. I did not know that, he said (though he knew very well what dropping contractions did to his voice). The ribbon metaphor was nice, he said then. Although I might've said tailor's table instead of seamstress's scissors. It doesn't exactly roll off the tongue, does it? *Seam-stresses. Seam-stress-is.* Not sure the pro-woman slant is worth it. But otherwise good work.

It was the *otherwise good work* that had put her over the edge. Well, *pro-woman slant* followed by *otherwise good work*. It was what he wrote at the end of a student critique when he felt he'd been too harsh: *Derivative, unintelligent, inarticulate, and a week late, but otherwise good work!* Nathan couldn't bear the idea that a student—even one of the idiots—should be angry at him.

Lady detectrix is redundant, she heard herself saying. She'd done her best to rein her voice in, keep it casual, as if this could hide the fact that Nathan's barb had found its mark, or that she'd been unable to think of a comeback when he'd said it an hour ago. As far as that goes, there's pretty much no way to say *detectrix* without sounding like an asshole. And *sleuth-sayer*, she added before Nathan could cut her off, is a Peplerism.

The term came by way of Roth, whom Nathan loved for the way he wrote about men but hated for the way he wrote about Jews, and Ellen loved for the way he wrote about writing but hated for the way he wrote about women. "The writer should be restrained from spilling the beans before they are digested," one-time quiz wiz and aspiring writer Alvin Pepler says in *The Anatomy Lesson*, and demands of enervated novelist Nathan Zuckerman an opinion of both the sentiment and its expression. Ellen and Nathan used to love to quote Zuckerman's response verbatim: "As serious and uncondescending a man of letters as there could ever be, Zuckerman said, 'I wonder if it's worth the effort.'" In the early days of their relationship Alvin Pepler had been Ellen and Nathan's go-to for the aspirational, self-consciously literary prose manufactured by most of the college's visiting writers. Pepler had served them faithfully through four years of endowed lectures and department meetings and conferences both home and away, had allowed them to mock neurotic novelists and pious poets to their faces until the day Nathan used his name to characterize one of her own stories. Ellen was still an adjunct at the time, a one-time visiting writer whose popularity with the students and faculty (in particular the up-and-coming editor of the relaunched *IGNIS* magazine) had prompted the department to find her one or two classes to teach each semester: a freshman comp roundup no one wanted, an intro to literary theory, the occasional workshop. In other words: it stung when Nathan used the term against her. Not like a bee sting (or a wasp's, or even a goddamn manta's) but like a home invasion, a long con: it was as if she'd returned to her house to find every-thing gone including her husband, who'd been playing her this whole time, pretending to be something he wasn't so he could steal all she owned.

In the car, Nathan had let her insult hang in the air for a moment (she, on the other hand, when he'd said it to her, had immediately thrown the printout of her story in the trash—a sym-bolic gesture, since they both knew the file remained on her computer). He'd closed his book and turned his phone face up and scrolled his way through his email or Facebook or one of the celebrity blogs he claimed he didn't read; tapped out what couldn't have been more than five words and laughed at his own cleverness and put the phone in the glove compartment and closed it. And then, a mile or two later: *Abusus non tollit usum.* Delivered in his Kosher-Canyon-by-way-of-Cambridge accent, consonants clipped but vowels just the teensiest bit nasal, as Paul said once ("Nasal" is a synonym for "Jewish," Nathan told her, when Ellen told him what her brother had said, as if that hadn't been the very reason why she'd tattled), and leaving Ellen with the damned-if-she-did, damned-if-she-didn't choice of asking Nathan if he'd known what abuses-whatever-whatever meant before they got in the car, or if he'd just now culled it from Wikipedia's List of Latin Phrases. By the time they arrived at Popham Beach they hadn't been speaking to each other, and in many ways they never resumed the habit when they got back to Saratoga.

Fast forward three years and here they were. Or, rather, here she was, at Popham Beach finally, but on her own. No family, no Nathan, no—

No, she said firmly, cutting short the pity parade. No no *no*.

She was about to head inside—maybe a shower would accomplish what Jackie's coffee hadn't—when a glint of light in the grass caught her eye. She smiled then, lingered a moment longer at the railing. The sparkle reflected off a sun-blanched soda or beer bottle—no one remembered which, if in fact any of the Baldwins had ever known. A good part of the family discussion around the vessel concerned whether it pre- or post-dated their tenancy of the Popham Beach house. Ellen insisted Paul had thrown it there when he was seven and she four, but over the course of thirty-plus years any memory of the incident had faded from her mind, and at this point she clung to her story solely for the sake of consistency. The bottle was part family joke, part family treasure; the fact that no one had ever trod across the protected patch of dune to remove it was less a testament to environmental ideals than to the fact that it provided an opportunity for the Baldwin men and women to act out one of their most beloved passion plays. At least once every summer, over an after-sailing before-dinner martini, Paul and their father (and later Nathan and Jackie's husband, William) talked about rigging up some kind of telescoping Chaplin spike to fish the bottle out, maybe borrow the Wilsons' pool skimmer, see if that would reach. But then Ellen and Jackie would protest, backed eventually by Paul's wife, Lane, and Jackie's girls, Chloe and Alison, little Paul always taking the men's side, their mother abstaining in the kitchen. If the discussion hadn't dissipated by the time Paul poured the adults their second martinis then Ellen would tromp to the bookcase and pull out the mold-spotted copy of Wallace Stevens and read aloud the "Anecdote of the Jar." One of the men would point out that the object in the grass was a *bottle*, not a *jar*, another would object that Popham Beach wasn't *exactly* the Tennessee frontier, but in the end Paul, first alone, later echoed by his son, would start chanting, Keep *of* the grass, keep *of* the grass: Lady Ellen was the Baldwin family's keeper of the grass, and if Lady Ellen wanted the bottle to stay, it stayed, like the mislettered signs and unconnected phone jacks and bricks of salt in the cabinets.

But Nathan, it seemed, wasn't going to stay.

The shock of it hit Ellen for the first time that morning. Not the ongoing series of spats and squabbles that had characterized their relationship since the beginning—and that she'd always rationalized as intellectually stimulating, a bit of barbed repartee to keep the fangs sharp or a way of venting steam so the pressure didn't build to an explosion—but its simpering end, no less surprising for being totally predictable. The pain was physical and sharp, like a Chaplin spike in her gut, so violent that she actually hunched forward, spilling cold coffee over her fingers. She flung the remainder of the liquid in the grass (a twinge of guilt, followed by a twinge of don't-be-ridiculous-Ellen) and went inside to get a rag to clean the deck planks, but as she passed the old

leather sofa in the living room she sank into it (a flash of the summer it migrated here, jutting out from either side of the car's roof
like a bicorne—her father's image, natch; the three children pos-
ing for a picture up top like the Beverly Hillbillies—also her
father's idea, surprisingly). She pulled the sofa's dustcover around
her shoulders. The radio was broadcasting something melan-
cholic, neoclassical, Britten maybe. No, Barber, that goddamn
Adagio for Strings. She could feel the musicians' bows slide across
their cellos and violins as though they raked over her own arms
and legs. It had felt a little like that last night, incredibly painful
yet almost sickeningly elegant too, as Nathan eloquently eviscer-
ated the past ten years of her life. With the same passionate yet
rational lucidity with which he might have flayed Milton's "Lyci-
das" or Tennyson's "In Memoriam" to one of his by-invite-only
seminars, Nathan had outlined the death of their marriage, detail-
ing the "insurmountable barriers" to their "renewed happiness,"
not the least of which turned out to be Lucy Watkins, a visiting
writer who'd been teaching an oversubscribed poetry workshop
for the past three semesters, and sleeping with Nathan for nearly
as long. With an almost horrific sense of detachment, Ellen noted
that Nathan spoke for exactly fifty minutes, at the end of which
he headed for the door with a brown leather suitcase only slightly
larger than the valise he carried to and from the classroom. The
idea that Nathan thought he could vet her from his life in the same
space of time he might devote to the hog-slaughtering scene in
Jude the Obscure so infuriated her that she snatched the car keys
from his hand and took off herself. By reflex she grabbed her
purse from the table in the foyer, but that was all she had: no

clothes, no books, none of the papers she was expected to hand back, graded, Monday morning.

The *Adagio* ended. There was a respectful pause, as if in remembrance of the war dead, and in the second of silence between the final decrescendo and a male voice overarticulating, That was Sam-u-el Bar-ber, Ellen heard a faint call through the open doors:

Todd, you motherfucker!

She almost laughed, instead started coughing when she inhaled the dust trapped in the blue-ticked sheet wrapped around her shoulders. Wearing the dustcover like a cloak, she made her way back to the deck. Four male figures in wetsuits were walking south down the beach. Three of them carried boogie boards and one held a long white surfboard under his arms, across his back, so that when he turned toward the ocean he looked (no other simile would do) like an angel with outstretched wings; another, noticeably rounder than his three companions and lagging behind them, carried a big white cooler slung over one shoulder. From this distance it was difficult to tell the walkers' age—they could be thirteen or thirty—but from the messiness of their hair and the slight aimlessness of their gait Ellen thought they had to be teenagers. Townies, of course. It was too late in the year for weekenders. Their pale faces sat atop their black-suited bodies like lanterns, and occasionally one of them would stoop over something on the beach and exclaim Ew, gross! (perhaps it was the thing that smelled so bad, Ellen thought, catching another whiff of it) or would pick up a pebble and clock one of the others. She assumed they were pebbles—either that or the fat boy was an actor flinching from laser beams that would be added in post. The fat boy, Ellen learned, was the one who'd called Todd a motherfucker when he—the fat boy, not Todd—called Michael a bitch. Michael was the boy with the surfboard. Ellen watched until the fat boy's roly-poly form disappeared behind the sharp cut where beach met bluffs south of the house. Her inner teacher told her it was wrong to mock, but really, the tubes of flesh inside the boy's wetsuit made him look like a rubber chew toy.

When she turned to go back inside she saw, just to the right of the French doors, a plastic yellow cat food dish. A few grains of sand lay in each of the dish's double compartments, and one of them was also encrusted with a dried brown residue. The dish had been tacked to the deck's planking, which smacked of her mother's thoroughness. Ellen could picture her mother coaxing some tent-shouldered tabby or calico onto the deck with a bit of left-over steak; and then the cans of cat food flashed in her mind. If she knew her mother, she wouldn't have stopped there. She'd have bought the animal a flea collar, taken it to get its shots, had it spayed or neutered. It was just how her mother did things. When Ellen was eight, Mrs. Baldwin had once made her husband turn the car around an hour outside of Worcester and drive all the way back home so she could post a birthday card she'd left on the table in the front hall. The incident was legendary in the Baldwin family, even though the identity of the recipient of the card, like the provenance of the bottle in the dune grass, had long since been forgotten. There was a right way and a wrong way to live your life, her mother always said. Call it the corollary to her father's core Baldwin belief, the praxis to the theory: you might only be able to understand the present through an understanding of past and future, but you could only *experience* it by going about your business as if time didn't exist. Ellen supposed the current buzzword was *mindfulness*, or maybe it had passed on to *living in the now*—she heard both terms at least once a week in yoga, something else she'd done a lot of the past three years—but her mother just called it *paying attention* (although put a couple of drinks in her and she started calling it *living* in a way that let you know she didn't think too many people knew how to do it as well as she did). It was a philosophy that had driven each of the Baldwin children crazy at one time or another, yet none of them could deny that their mother was not only successful but happy. She'd managed to hold onto her job at a Boston-based publishing company through two decades of mergers that made it part of the third-largest multimedia corporation in the world, only to resign after being asked to edit the self-serving autobiography of a tobacco industry executive; and she'd held on to her husband as well, a semi-retired professor of American history so disinvested in the now that the Baldwin children were convinced he'd written all of his second and wildly unsuccessful book (*Pottery Without the Wheel: The Technological Successes and Failures of Native North Americans*) at the dinner table. But, as Jackie had once observed, their mother never seemed troubled by silence on the part of a conversational partner. If anything, she preferred it.

Ellen bent down now, flicked the little plastic dish. It responded with a timpani-like sound. The pale red polish on her nails, she saw, was cracked from six hours of biting at them on the road last night. The gnawed polish chastened her a little—a vile habit, her mother always said, painting your nails—but the dish hurt more. It had obviously been a part of Popham Beach for a while, and she had not. In fact, she'd only seen the family twice in the past year, at Christmas and at Easter, and the latter only because it coincided with Skidmore's spring break. It had been Nathan's idea they go, she remembered now—and then he'd gotten sick the day before the trip. Well, she supposed she knew what *sick* meant. And now look at her: bending over a cat food dish and flicking it with nails as chipped as the potsherds on her father's shelf and wearing a dustcover as a housecoat—which, she saw when she looked down, was soaking up the coffee she'd spilled a few minutes ago.

Sighing, she walked to the kitchen to rinse the sheet out, then dropped it in the washer instead, peeled off the stale-smelling clothes she'd driven up in and dropped them in as well. She set the machine to cold so her bra and undies wouldn't come out pink, added soap, then let the lid fall closed with a bang. The washing machine was old and filled slowly, hissing loudly as though steam instead of water bled into the tub. After a few minutes the hissing stopped and something inside the machine clicked—Ellen could feel the ratchet's pop in her right hand, still resting on the washer's lid—and then the whole machine began to vibrate wildly as the drum and agitator began spinning. Jackie and Paul's children loved to clamber aboard the washer when it shook like this, as the Baldwin children had loved the quarter rides in front of the A&P when they were young, but it wasn't until Ellen smiled at the memory that she tasted salt and realized she was crying. Why now? was one of the few things she'd managed to say to Nathan last night. You said it's been going on for a year and a half. So what made you decide to tell me now? For the only time the whole evening Nathan's oratorical skills had failed him. Lucy . . . she's . . . His mouth couldn't give shape to the words but his hands did, holding it there like a sack of flour in front of his belly. No, Ellen had to admit. Not a sack but a pillow, a beach ball—something light, unburdensome, comfortable even. Nathan had shrugged then, but it was a hard shrug, as if he were shirking off his momentary wavering. It's due in March, he said. I want this over by then. I want it to have my name.

Ellen, naked, shivering in the cold kitchen, laid her head on the rattling machine as if it could shake the sobs from her, and it did. She could hear her wails over the machine's rattle, feel its enameled surface grow slick with her tears. She sobbed and punched the hollow machine as if it and not Nathan had taken from her the illusion of her marriage, the possibility of bringing her own child to Popham Beach and holding his or her hand as they waded into the ocean, listening to his or her screams as the washer bucked him or her—*it!*—to and fro. She allowed herself a neat eighteen minutes of squalor and then, when the washer clicked again and fell silent, so did she. Beneath her cheek something sighed as the water began to drain from the tub, but Ellen felt dried out already. She stood up and wiped her face. She noticed the chill in the kitchen again, noticed also that she was naked. Jesus Christ, she said out loud, glancing through the open doors to the deck and the grass and the beach beyond. She wrapped her arms around her chest half in modesty, half in warmth, trotted upstairs to the bathroom and cranked both handles of the shower all the way open. The old pipes spat first, a little air, a little rust, and then a flood of clean warm water cascaded out of the oxidized spigot. Water and water and water, she thought, stepping into the tub. The ocean, the washer, her tears, the first two somehow producing the last. And now the shower, to wash her tears away. Water, water everywhere. Ellen stood under the warm stream for a good twenty-five minutes, not washing, just spinning slowly and letting the water erode what it could from her back, her breasts, her left shoulder, her right, imagining her body whittled down to a bony pillar, a cross between one of the hoodoos up the beach and the kaolin pipe in her father's study. When the water started to go cold she turned it off and toweled herself dry and combed her hair, located in Jackie's closet a blanched blue sweatshirt embroidered with a frayed golden lobster and, in Paul's dresser, a pair of institutional gray sweatpants—the institution was Harvard, though the crimson H had long since abraded away—then headed downstairs to hang her clothes up. On the way out of Paul's room she caught a glimpse of herself in the mirror, sweatshirt sleeves pushed to her forearms, sweatpants rolled above stubbled ankles. Good god woman, she said, flashing her nails in the glass to reveal—revel in—the full horror. You look like a townie.

Downstairs, the clothesline drooped off the summer beam like Christmas garland, and as Ellen pinned her things up she remembered the day her father had first told her the name of the massive wooden joist spanning the house's central axis, studded here and there by rusted iron hardware still bearing the imprint of the hammer blows that had pounded it into shape almost two centuries earlier, along with hooks and bolts and O-rings that could have held oil lamps or cast-iron kettles or a person. A fucking bondage lover's *dream*, Paul had quipped, but the story Ellen preferred was the first one, the day she'd learned the beam had its own name. This wasn't a story like the story of the bottle in the dune. She could picture the event clearly, hear her father speak to her in his lecturer's voice. *Summer*, from Old English *sumter*, meaning "pack animal" or "saddle-bearer"; or, alternately, *sommier*, the French for "rafter." She'd been eight; her father had stood on the three-legged milking stool she stood on now; and as she handed him one piece of wet clothing at a time he told her how the house's post-and-beam construction rendered it a hollow shell whose only internal support was the summer beam spanning its width and, Atlas-like, shouldering the entire weight of the second story. Without it, he said, the house would collapse in on itself. Ellen, a little confused, a little distracted by the ickiness of handling grown-up underpants (or maybe, though she was loath to admit it, simply preferring her own version of things), had thought her father was referring not to the wood above his head but to the shaft of cathedral sunlight pouring through the leaded-glass window behind him. The light *seemed* solid, and it was easy to imagine that it held up the sleeping Baldwins in their bedrooms the same way a few grains of sand and strands of grass held back the ocean. Even after she'd realized her error (or conceded her folly, she might confess after one of Paul's martinis, or two), she persisted in thinking of the summer beam as both insubstantial and solid, and later that year, when she saw shafts of Jesus light pushing through dissolving clouds over Popham Beach and the vast ocean beyond, she thought all of Heaven must rest upon those summer beams as on stilts.

Cathedral windows, Jesus light, summer beams: to Ellen they were anthropomorphic substitutes for a faith whose loss had, she always assumed, predated not just her generation but her parents', symbolic connections to rituals and beliefs that were becoming progressively more secular and empty as time went on. Or so she'd thought until last Christmas, when her parents had announced, as if it were no more remarkable than the presence of ham on the table instead of turkey, that they were off to mass at St. Anthony's, and did any of the children want to join them? The children, who had half a dozen masses between them, had demurred, and had spent the past ten months trying to figure out what had brought their parents back to the fold. Pop-cultural Paul suggested the *fin-du-monde* fantasies associated with the Mayan calendar and the year 2012, even though their father specialized in North American indigenous cultures. Philosophical Jackie went with impending mortality, even though both of their parents, as they themselves put it, had been born fifty, and refused to age a day since. In fact the question hadn't really concerned Ellen until she'd confided to her mother at Easter that she and Nathan were having problems. *Confided* wasn't quite the right word, since she'd had to raise the subject three or four times before her mother finally responded. Well, frankly dear, I'm not surprised, Mrs. Baldwin said without looking up from the dishes she washed and handed to Ellen to dry. Your father and I always thought you had no business marrying a Jew.

VIII.

He said: Fiction is an argument against good taste and practicality. He said: The best novelists are half-baked philosophers, obsessive-compulsive neurotics who see the shape of the universe in Whitman's leaf of grass. Take the sentiment: "I believe a leaf of grass is no less than the journey-work of the stars." It turns on its misuse, perhaps misunderstanding, of the word journeywork, which refers to mundane actions performed by apprentices and not to the journeying of stars—which is another error, since stars are fixed in place, and it's only our perspective from an orbiting, rotating planet that causes them to seem to move. Melville thought whales were fish; Proust thought homosexual men were female souls trapped in men's bodies. Faulkner believed goodness to be the unique provenance of post-menopausal mammies. It's these irrational opinions, he said, these misuses of rhetoric and vocabulary, that give fiction its power. Fiction is an argument for its own necessity, he said. A story—this story—is nothing but a brick, a cinderblock, a stone in that great big wall writer and reader build together. Pick it up, he said, mount the scaffolding, climb all the way to the top and lay it in place. And while you're up there, he said, take one last look around, because the scaffolding comes down now and this is your last glimpse of freedom. Or don't, he said. He said: Don't build the wall. Refuse to build the wall. He said: Call it a chair instead. He said: You can sit down instead. You can rest, he said. At long last, he said, you can rest.

"During their courtship Stan laid it on thick, gilding his lilies with a can of Krylon, and if Shirl was put off by the smell she was also attracted to the color, and soon enough allowed herself to be plucked."

This was the sentence that had ended Ellen and Nathan's marriage, even if it had taken six years of internal, invisible erosion before the exterior edifice finally collapsed in on itself. It wasn't a particularly good sentence—it was, in fact, Ellen's private parody of the famous line from *Goodbye, Columbus*, which she felt the post-*Portnoy* Roth (or at least Nathan Zuckerman) would've found a tad Pepleresque: "We whipped our strangeness and newness into a froth that resembled love, and we dared not play too long with it, talk too much of it, or it would flatten and fizzle away." Ellen's gloss appeared in an unfinished book she'd tried to write about the novelist Shirley Jackson's marriage to the critic Stanley Edgar Hyman, in particular the dislocating experience of being a woman writer and urbane intellectual—married to a Jewish Communist, no less—in rural Vermont. In the hundred or so pages Ellen had managed to write she'd painted Jackson as a latter-day Virginia Woolf, a brilliant but neurotic female artist who hid behind her husband, but also manipulated him into playing second fiddle to her in the professional sphere; she supposed Joan Didion was a more recent example of the type. The parallels to her and Nathan were obvious enough, but so, she'd assumed, were the differences; which, looking back, is probably what gave her the freedom to cast the relationship in such a negative light. Her Stan wasn't a particularly attractive man—Hyman had been no beauty either—and he relied on a combination of self-mockery and unctuous flattery to win Shirl's hand, if not her heart. I mean, *gilding, Krylon, lilies, plucked.* Nathan flicked each word hard enough to leave the impression of his fingernail in the paper. It's straining a little bit, don't you think? For effect? It's supposed to be funny, Ellen said. It's Stan who's straining, not the prose. Stan's a little too close to Nathan Pepler if you ask me. Alvin, Nathan added a moment later. Alvin Pepler.

I should've just called him Nathan, Ellen thought to herself—this was around one, in the middle of her third (and decidedly unmindful) sun salutation. Nate and El. But that's where the comparison broke down. Nathan was the genius in their relationship, or at least the one who put his work out there and received accolades for it, whereas Ellen was lucky to publish one or two stories a year, and all too often in *IGNIS*, in the back third of the book, which Nathan had once referred to as the "Friends and Family" section. There was no "Lottery" in her oeuvre, no "Charles" for that matter. No children. No "business on earth," as Hawthorne had written on the birth of his daughter. But at least there was coffee: she'd driven to Phippsburg after her shower, bought real coffee and milk, pasta in boxes and sauce in jars, on impulse a couple of six packs of beer. She'd thought about calling her mother but had been saved by a weak signal on her cell (she wasn't looking forward to a triumphant reiteration of "the Jew line," as she and Jackie had dubbed it, but she was even more put off by the idea of having it come over a staticky connection—of having to ask her mother to repeat it). Upon her return to the house she'd made coffee, lunch; eaten and washed dishes; uncovered the furniture and folded up the dustcovers. She'd bought nail polish remover as well, polish, cuticle scissors, emery board, and spent forty-five minutes giving herself a manicure (taking off her wedding ring when she reached that finger, then putting it back on again, then taking it off and putting it on the windowsill where with any luck a magpie might come along and steal it). She puzzled through three or four beautifully abstruse Stevens lyrics while her nails dried but kept seeing her own situation in the words. When she got to that line she cast aside the sea-swollen pages, exchanged the sweatshirt for a swim-suit top, and attempted a little yoga on the deck. The top was Jackie's. Like the decaf, it was a relic of her last pregnancy, when her sister's breasts had swollen by two full cup sizes, and when Ellen bent over her own breasts flopped out of the hollow navy-blue triangles and she laughed unreservedly for the first time that morning. She retied the top more tightly around her neck and stepped stiffly through the poses, wondering why on earth they were called sun salutations, when if you actually looked at the sun while doing them you were blinded and lost your balance and fell over—and if you looked down, you saw a yellow cat food dish, equally distracting. The hardest part, though, was the pranayama, which seemed to bring lungfuls of whatever smelled so fetid deep into her body.

She was holding a half-hearted warrior pose when she heard the fat boy's voice—what was his name again, Michael? or was

Michael the boy with the surfboard?—pierce the sound of the waves. Fucking say that again and I'll fucking kill your faggot ass dead. She took a moment to tighten the sagging swimsuit top before going to the railing and looking out at the beach. The three lean boys, she saw, had peeled open the tops of their wetsuits in the afternoon heat, and the one with the surfboard—Ellen was pretty sure he was the one called Michael—had shifted his board atop his head as though it were a gigantic wimple. The sleeves of the lean boys' wetsuits dragged in the sand and their heads were slick domes now. Only the fat boy still wore his wetsuit zippered up to his neck, still lugged his cooler, though now it bounced emptily off his plump behind. The cooler reminded Ellen of the beer in the fridge. She asked herself if she'd bought it with the boys in mind—certainly she preferred wine to beer, and there was sure to be several bottles in the pantry under the stairs—but even as she pondered the implications of this idea the boy with the surfboard on his head turned onto the path that led to the Baldwins' house. The board turned with him in a ninety-degree arc like a helicopter blade warming up, and its fin nearly smacked the boy behind him. Goddammit, Michael, the second boy said as he too turned onto the Baldwins' property. Watch the fuck out.

But Michael didn't answer. He was, instead, looking at her, and after a long pause Ellen heard a wolf whistle float across the grass. Michael, the boy whose name she thought was Michael said, shut your fucking cake hole before I feed you this board. Fuck *you*, Michael, the fat boy said. I'll whistle at the bitch if I want to. The boy with the surfboard—were they *both* named

Michael?—whipped around so fast it seemed the spinning surfboard was going to lift him off the ground. He said something, what, Ellen didn't hear, and the fat boy said, Fuck you again, but so quietly she barely heard him. Then the boy with the surfboard turned again and led the others up the path to the deck. He made eye contact with Ellen, smiling at her brightly, and even at that distance, with his features obscured by the surfboard's shadow, Ellen could see how good-looking he was. He knew it too, his smile all cocked up on the left side as if to say, hey, I can't help that I'm so fucking cute.

The other two shirtless boys would only glance at her covertly, while the fat boy kept his eyes on the path in front of his trudging feet. They walked all the way up to the deck and climbed the stairs before saying anything, and then the boy holding the surfboard on his head took a hand off it to wave and say, What's up? His smile had leveled out a little, become a little less cocksure, and Ellen's mind flashed on the six-packs of beer and the whole *Summer of '42* potential of the scene—the kid was really, really cute—before she offered him a wry smile and said, Not much.

I'm Michael, the boy with the surfboard said. My compadres here are Todd, Sony, and the fat one is called Michael too.

Fuck you, Michael, the fat boy said.

Michael too, Ellen repeated. As in *Michael also*, or *Michael Number Two*?

Confusion clouded the eyes of the boy with the surfboard, and then he smiled it away. As the lady prefers. Todd and Sony usually call him Fat Michael, to distinguish him from me. The curved tip of his nodding surfboard dipped down like a bird pecking at seed.

Fuck you, Michael, the fat boy said again, his cheeks red with exertion but his voice flat, unimpassioned. Fuck you too, Todd, he said when one of the other boys snickered.

Thin Michael turned now, and the other three boys scattered before his revolving board. The teacher in her asserted itself.

Why don't you put that thing down before you take out someone's eye?

Does that mean you're inviting us to stay? Thin Michael said, smiling as he took the board off his head. He looked around the deck, then walked toward the railing. Ellen thought he was going to lean it against a post but instead he lifted it over the top rail and drove it into the grass.

Hey, not the—but she was cut off by the board's sharp tail slicing through sand and root.

Without the board on his head Ellen could see Thin Michael's face more clearly, tanned even complexion and shoulder-length blond hair, dry strands of which were beginning to come unstuck from the back of his neck in pale gold curls. He had a long straight nose, sharp enough to open a letter on, and his eyes were very, very blue. What was Flaubert's metaphor for Madame Bovary's eyes? China blue, or the color of a certain flower? Or was it that Emma's eyes kept changing color? The boy's were stable enough, brilliant but without depth or texture, like pieces of polished, unveined turquoise.

She realized she was staring and felt the blood rush to her cheeks. To cover, she stuck her arm out awkwardly and walked toward Thin Michael, practically shouting her name as if she were deep into the second hour of some interminable faculty party.

Thin Michael didn't say anything, but his fingers were hot and damp around hers, his grip light but definite. For a moment Ellen thought he was going to bow and kiss the back of her hand.

Another snicker from one of the boys. Ellen felt Thin Michael's fingers squeeze hers, then relax. The pleasure is all mine, he said in the self-mocking yet somehow genuine voice of his generation. He was still looking at her and smiling broadly when he added, Todd, if you make that vulgar noise one more time I'm going to knock your fucking teeth so far down your throat you'll be picking them out of your shit for the next two weeks.

Fat Michael laughed so hard he choked, and Ellen took the opportunity to withdraw her hand, also hot now, and damp, from Thin Michael's. She caught a glimpse of her freshly painted nails. Todd's face, she saw then, had gone as red as her nail polish, but his Fuck you, Michael, seemed directed at the fat one and not the one who still stood in front of her, smiling his cocksure smile and staring at her with those goddamn gorgeous blue eyes.

Ellen dried her hands on Paul's sweatpants. So, um, you guys look hot, she said, and ignored Todd's muffled snicker. Can I offer you a drink or something? Water, soda, I think there might be some beer in the fridge?

There was a hollow thump as Fat Michael's cooler fell to the floor of the deck.

Hot damn. Beer.

Thin Michael smiled apologetically. Forgive the uncouth manners of my friends and Fat Michael, he said, but their experience of real women is limited to their mothers' titties, cousins' panties, and certain floozies of, shall we say, the two-dimensional persuasion. Please, allow me to graciously—no, *gratefully*—accept your offer of cold brewskis on their behalf.

Despite herself, Ellen guffawed.

Okay, slugger, turn it down. My husband just left me and I need a little distraction, but if I wanted a dose of the effects of polyvalent cultural hybridization on the speech patterns of contemporary youth I'd attend a literary conference or turn on MTV. I bought Corona, she added as she headed into the house. You boys want limes?

Yes, please, Thin Michael said, his meekness as self-indulgent as everything else about him. There was another snicker, and Ellen heard the sound of fist on flesh.

Ow, she heard someone, presumably Todd, say. Fuck you, Michael.

I'm sorry to hear about your marital difficulties, Thin Michael called as she cut the lime into wedges. Does this mean your husband isn't accompanying you on your present holiday?

Ellen almost sliced the tip of her thumb off. She looked across the living room to the deck. Thin Michael wasn't looking at her, but was bent over and examining the cat food dish. She gathered the necks of the five beers in her red-tipped fingers and headed back outside.

Um, *no*, she said, trying not to sound too sarcastic. My husband did not accompany me on my present *holiday*.

The boys had leaned their boogie boards against the railing and arranged themselves in the deck chairs Ellen had carried up from the basement when she got back from the grocery store. As she bent over to set the beers on the low table she had a distinct sense of her breasts swinging a little too freely in Jackie's swimsuit top, and she pretended not to notice four pairs of teenaged eyes staring at them.

Thin Michael's smile was thin, inscrutable. A woman should have her family with her at moments like this, he said, pulling at his beer.

My parents close the house on Labor Day, Ellen said, more curtly then she'd intended. They're retired. They bought a camper and're making a tour of the sites of alleged North American miracles. *So*, she continued, louder, when Thin Michael opened his mouth, are you boys in college or something?

Sony slammed his beer down on the table. Fuck *college*. College is so *last century*.

Ellen started, not at the sound but at the term, which was one of Nathan's favorites, e.g., "As the last century hastened to its close, a new generation of post-colonial writers enormously expanded the vocabulary, rhythms, and indeed the very frontiers of the English novel." Ellen had once asked Nathan why he never talked about *this* century, and he'd answered so quickly that she knew he'd prepared his response ahead of time: This century hasn't started yet. The oughties were just the 2-0-C's unfinished business. Later, scrolling through the comments on one of his pieces in *IGNIS*, she found the same answer posted in reply to a reader who'd referred to his analysis as "dated" (with the exception of "2-0-C," which Nathan had lifted from his critic).

Fucking global *recession*, man, Todd said now. Fucking Iraq. Fucking *Barry*'s practically invited the fucking *Muslims* to blow this shit *up*.

Barry? Ellen wondered, wracking her brain for a possible ref-
erent. Manilow? Diller? Dave Barry? J.M. Barrie? Did these boys
fancy themselves Lost in some Peter Pannish way? But then she
realized they were referring to the president by his childhood
nickname. She supposed they'd read *The Audacity of Hope* in a
class, but coming from Todd it sounded like the kind of detail an
assassin would memorize while studying his target.

Fucking 9/11 part *deux*, Sony said, grabbing his bottle and
knocking it into Todd's hard enough to make Ellen wince.
Memento mori, boys. We are all about to fucking *die*.

Another flash: Ellen had been on the phone with her father
that morning, who told her before it happened that the towers
were going to fall. The modern skyscraper is basically a post-and-
beam affair, he'd said almost with interest. A hollow shell, all
exoskeleton. It's the same theory as the beach house, with the
individual floors acting as the summer beam. Take away enough
of them and the structure is bound to implode.

College is next year, Thin Michael said. We're all seventeen.
We're seniors.

Seniors rule! Fat Michael called out, raising his fist. Yeah! He
held his arm in the air for a moment, then let it fall to his lap.

Shut up, Michael, Todd said, and a took a drink. You fucking
loser.

Both Todd and the boy they called Sony had faces like whip-
pets mounted atop the dangerously thin bodies of hyperactive
teenaged boys. Their arms were as knotted as a ship's anchor
rope, their chests as flat as the underside of a china platter save
for a central channel that seemed impressed into the skin by a

potter's thumb. By contrast, Thin Michael's limbs were more rounded, generous. His waist was delicate and soft as a kouros boy's but his chest and arms had thickened with his burgeoning manhood. Speaking of which: Ellen couldn't help but notice that when Thin Michael propped his legs on the railing a thick ripple appeared in his wetsuit, stretching from his crotch halfway to his knee. Ellen assumed it was an air pocket in the neoprene, or else the boy had a penis the size of a paper towel tube.

Ripples, unfortunately, were all Fat Michael seemed to have, from his double chin to the cleft sag of his chest to the parallel folds that ribbed his stomach. He sat back from the other boys, holding his beer in both hands and sipping at it so slowly that Ellen could almost hear him tallying the calories in his head and wondering why a Todd or Sony could guzzle theirs with impunity. Her pity must have shown itself on her face, because when Fat Michael's eyes caught hers he directed at her a look of such disgust that she physically recoiled.

That fucking *stinks*, Fat Michael said, but before Ellen could apologize—what the hell have I got myself *into*, she thought—Fat Michael got up and walked to the railing. Smells like something *died* in your backyard.

The wind was coming in off the water, and Ellen smelled it too.

Oh, um, yes. I, um, noticed it before. Sorry.

Allow me, Thin Michael said.

What?

Before Ellen could stop him, Thin Michael had set his beer down and vaulted to the grass.

Hey, you really shouldn't—

Wow, Thin Michael cut her off, it's a *lot* worse down here. There was an odd gap between words and tone, as if Thin Michael wasn't bothered by the smell at all, but looking forward to finding a particularly grisly corpse.

Ellen heaved herself off her chair. Though she'd only had three or four sips of beer, she felt oddly light-headed as she made her way to the deck railing.

You really shouldn't be down there. You'll damage the grass.

Thin Michael was crouching down, peering under the deck.

Hey, Sony. Gimme Fat Michael's boogie board.

Aw, Michael, fuck you, dude, Fat Michael said. He tried to head off Sony as he went for his board but the lighter boy danced around him. He tossed the board to Todd first—just to make Fat Michael jump, Ellen thought—and then Todd tossed it to Thin Michael in the grass.

Look, Ellen said, squatting down to bring her face closer to Thin Michael's. She pointed to the nearest sign. It's family policy. No one on the grass.

Thin Michael was probing with the boogie board under the deck. His action reminded Ellen of a pizza man reaching deep into an oven with his paddle.

I . . . think . . . I . . . He gave the board a sharp snap. Got it!

Ellen sighed, stood up. When she turned around, she saw that the other three boys were looking not at Thin Michael but at her, and she crossed her arms over her chest. For some reason the image of the boys turning onto the Baldwins' path came to her mind, and she had the feeling that they already knew what Thin Michael was going to pull out from under the porch.

He really shouldn't be down there. He'll damage the—She was going to say ecosystem, then changed her mind. Grass, she said again, shrugging.

Todd snickered.

Don't think I didn't hear that, Todd, Thin Michael said from behind Ellen.

When she turned she saw Thin Michael's chest first, corded with the effort of holding Fat Michael's boogie board level in front of him. Then she saw the cat on the end of the boogie board. Her first impression was that it was even skinnier than she'd imagined, but then she realized it was probably just rotted out. Hollow, and collapsing in on itself. There was the flea collar, pulled so deeply up and behind the jaw that Ellen thought the animal must've been hung by it, or perhaps swung round and round until its neck snapped.

Meow! Ellen heard right in her ear, and she turned to see that the three boys had crowded in close. It was Fat Michael who had meowed. That is one dead cat, he said with all the enthusiasm of a first-night moviegoer rating the slasher pic he's just seen.

Ellen could just make out the cat food dish between Fat Michael's shoulder and Sony's. Oh god, she said, feeling like she was going to throw up. Just get rid of it, she said, not looking back at Thin Michael, not caring about the grass. Just, I don't know, bury it or something. Make it go away.

She went to push her way through the boys but as she did the strap of her swimsuit caught on something and jerked to the right. It didn't come off but her breasts nearly fell out of the oversized cups. She thought she must have snagged it on the zipper pull of one of the boy's wetsuits, but as she reached to unsnag herself she saw that it had in fact caught on Fat Michael's finger.

Meow, Fat Michael said again.

She turned to run but Todd was there, his chest every bit as hard as it looked. It vibrated when she collided with him, but held firm. He pushed her backwards and then there were hands on both her arms propelling her faster. The railing caught her in the small of the back and then her legs were in the air over her head. She opened her mouth to scream but the ground was there faster and harder than she would have expected. It seemed as if the breath rushed out of her pores as well as her mouth, and she lay on the grass flat as a popped balloon. It was only when she smelled the cat that she realized she was breathing. She saw dark shapes falling out of the sky—the boys leaping after her, blurry black-and-white forms in their half-open wetsuits.

Let's get her away from this stink, she heard Thin Michael say. It's making me want to puke.

She felt her arms being lifted, her legs, but still couldn't find the strength to struggle. The grass was simultaneously coarse and sharp against the small of her back and she could feel sand sifting into the seat of Paul's sweatpants. She felt as if the weight of her body was cutting into the sand like a plow, imagined a channel opening in the dune where they dragged her, water rushing in where her body had ripped the grass out by its roots. The channel widening until the whole house floated away and all that was left behind were a few jagged promontories, the occasional book or bottle surfacing every few years like the sherds on her father's desk.

She found her limbs then, began to thrash. A foot caught Todd in his mouth and she saw blood spray from his lips. When Thin Michael reached for her throat she caught the side of his hand in her teeth. A big round shadow loomed on her right side, collapsed on her stomach. Thin Michael's hand flew from her mouth as Fat Michael's knee drove into her gut.

Jesus Christ, Thin Michael said. Fucking hold her still, will you?

I want to go first, Fat Michael said. I saw her first.

Fuck you, Michael, Thin Michael said. I did all the work. This one's mine.

Todd's face was right over Ellen's when she looked up, his snickering mouth full of blood. Then he and Sony pulled her arms away from her body while Thin Michael kicked her legs apart. The boys' hands were hot and soft and wet on her arms, in contrast with the sand under them, which was dry, coarse, cold. Ellen wanted to apologize to the dune, to say that this wasn't her fault, but she couldn't catch her breath since Fat Michael had fallen into her. She could see him in the background, watching like he always did, and it was him she hated, the fat fuck.

In the space marked out by Thin Michael and Todd and Sony's heads she could see the sky. The clouds were thicker now, a gray that was closer to black than it was to white. No light pulsed through the clouds, but she wondered if her parents' god were looking down through the gaps anyway. Did god distinguish between past and present and future, or was it all the same to him? A house, a hoodoo, a wilderness or a nation. She felt she must be invisible by now, but that he could still locate her by narrowing his gaze to the four signs marking the boundary between the manmade and natural worlds and zeroing in on the four boys until he'd interpolated her position. But what would he see? She felt she was nothing more than the space between them.

The boys' voices were harsh as gulls fighting over a bit of carrion as they cheered Thin Michael on. She had read about moments like this, had been told that in order for these boys to do what they were doing they had to deny her personality, her humanity. Now she realized that that was just another denial. They knew exactly who she was, what they were doing to her. It was she who had to disengage if she wanted to survive. Had to tell herself that the body these boys had commandeered was no more her than the Popham Beach house was her family. But she didn't believe that either. She didn't have her parents' faith, which is why it was the signs she'd worried about last night and the dunes she worried about now, why she looked to the sky for a sign that god existed but saw only her own gaze reflected back at her.

She heard a ripping sound but kept her eyes focused on the empty sky. The first time she'd seen crepuscular rays and thought of it as her father's summer beam, the Baldwins were just getting in to Popham Beach. It had rained almost the whole drive from Worcester, the storm only letting up sometime after Yarmouth, after which the single layer of cloud had begun to break apart into thick sun-edged tufts like gold-fringed pillows. By the time the car turned off 18 onto the puddley two-track that led to the Baldwins' house the clouds had pushed further apart and the sunlight beat down on the house in hard yellow bars. As she grew up, Ellen would come to see the light as softer, undulating like the bottom of a curtain or the ripple of flotsam on the beach or the sinewy lines of an Aalto vase, but that morning the light looked as hard as tent poles, and Ellen had thought her family's little saltbox would surely collapse beneath its weight. She had always believed faith must be that heavy, the incredible burden of supporting something that refused to reveal itself until you died. She imagined that that's what her parents were doing driving around America in their camper: not looking for miracles but looking for death, when what they should have been doing was looking out for her. But even as she thought that, her diaphragm spasmed, her gut contracted as if of its own accord, and all the air in her lungs rushed out in denial.

I PROTEST!

With a start, Thin Michael stopped his thrusting.

What'd she say?

The other boys looked at him strangely.

She didn't say nothing, Fat Michael said. Hurry up, it's getting late.

Thin Michael looked down at Ellen's face. She was staring up at the sky, her eyes as open and empty as her mouth. A foot away from her head he saw an empty bottle.

Maybe we should gag her, he said. If she keeps yelling someone might hear.

Whatever, Fat Michael said. Just hurry it up, I gotta be home for dinner.

Thin Michael propped himself on his right arm, reached with his left for the bottle half submerged in sand. The base of it was too wide to fit in Ellen's mouth so he flipped it, aimed the bottle's open mouth at hers. When he hesitated a few drops of liquid dribbled onto Ellen's chin.

C'mon, Todd said. Just pop it in there like a cork.

Make her suck that bottle like it was your dick, Sony said, and Todd said, Good one! and they high-fived each other.

Fat Michael raised a hand to get in on the action but when Todd and Sony left him hanging he let it fall instead on the back of the bottle in Thin Michael's hand. It missed Ellen's lips, teeth, slid past tongue and uvula until it lodged against her epiglottis. Spittle came out around the edges of the bottle and then mucus spurted from Ellen's nose in yellowish streaks and then Ellen's body bucked up and down.

Oh yeah, she's gagging on it! Todd said.

Fucking gag on it, bitch! Sony said.

When she'd settled down Thin Michael resumed his work, and it was only when he went to switch places with Fat Michael that he noticed something was wrong. Ellen's limbs seemed as stringy and empty as the cat's. He tried to pull the bottle from her mouth but it wouldn't come. He shook it with both hands but Ellen's head only flopped on the end of it like a fish on a hook, and when he dropped her back to the ground the bottle stuck straight up like a buoy. She's fine, right? Thin Michael said, backing away. She's fine, Fat Michael said, not caring about getting his turn. Better than she's ever been. It wasn't until a few hours after the boys left that the stretched skin of Ellen's cheeks began to slacken and the seal broke and the bottle fell back to the grass. Her mouth remained open though, distended in silence, and that evening, when it rained, it filled with a tiny pool of the same acidic drops that had, over the past quarter century, eroded the name from the bottle beside her head. In the trial against the boys it would be labeled "People's Exhibit A: Bottle (Original Contents Unknown)."

ABUSUS NON TOLLIT USUM: abuse does not remove use. In keeping with the Ashkenazi tradition of Nathan Miller's family, his son with Lucy Watkins, born on the Ides of March in the year 2012, was named Michael, after her brother, who was killed in the final days of American military activity in Iraq. *Si vis pacem, para bellum*. If it's peace you want, prepare for war.

—2010

IX.

I cut a piece from time once, when I was very young. Finger scissors, laser sight, and for some reason it was crucial to stick my tongue out like my father when he measured pipe. When I squeezed carelessly I felt something bend around my fingers like glossy paper resisting dull scissors, but when I concentrated, when I stiffened my index and middle fingers and moved them up and down in the same plane, I heard a sound like Jell-O sucking free from a mold and a hole opened up in the air, not so much black as blank, a void. My skin vacuumed itself to my bones as a giant hand squeezed the air from my lungs, and when the air cleared, all that was left was the cobwebby feel of a transparent sheet draped over my fingers. But no, not a sheet: a moment, four or five seconds long, just over half that in width. Ten, maybe fifteen seconds I could do anything with. I could step inside Leonardo's studio, say, and watch him paint the Mona Lisa's smile, or cut the brake line on Hitler's father's car, or slip into my mother's hospital room to tell her goodbye. For years I carried that moment on me, waiting for something to tell me now, *now is the time to use it*, and this, *this is the thing to use it for*. But nothing ever presented itself. Which is to say, a thousand things presented themselves, but none of them seemed worth sacrificing the others for. Sometimes the possibility of choice means more than something you can hold in your hands. And so, after a lifetime of false starts and backward glances, I've decided to surrender it to whomever chance delivers this. What I mean is, I wrote this note on it, but I wrote it on the back. All you have to do is turn the page.